LOCAL
HERO

LOCAL HERO

The Dunquin Cove Story

By

Rodney Riesel

Published by Island Holiday Publishing

East Greenbush, NY

Special thanks to:

Pamela Guerriere

Kevin Cook

Cover Image by:

Kim Seng at RoyalStockPhoto.com

Cover Design by:

Connie Fitsik

To learn about my other books friend me at

https://www.facebook.com/rodneyriesel

For Brenda,
Kayleigh, Ethan
& Peyton

Chapter One

Ben Dunning stared without expression over the top of his cards across the round, wooden table at Curt Holliday. Curt had a slight smirk on his face. Was he smirking because he had a great hand … or because he had nothing? Ben wondered.

"Come on, it's almost midnight," Sam O'Brien, the owner of The Cove Restaurant, groaned.

Ben glanced down at his chips, and then at the chips in front of the other four men. "I'm out," he said, and dropped his cards face down on the table. "What do you got?"

Curt laughed as he tossed his hand onto the stack of chips in the pot. "Nothing!"

"You bastard!" Ben shot back. "You smirk if you have something, you smirk if you don't. It's like playing cards with a grinning robot."

Curt raked his winnings toward himself with both hands. "What can I say? When I was in the Navy they called me Ol' Stone Face."

Artie pushed his chair back from the table. "You don't want to know what we call you around here."

"You takin' off, Artie?" John Morgan asked. He picked up his cigar from the ashtray and took a long drag. Then he tilted his head back, made an "O" with his mouth, and blew three perfect smoke rings. He figured his friends were envious of his talent. They weren't

"Yeah, I gotta get up early. It's supposed to rain tomorrow afternoon and I want to get some work done before it does." Artie stood, side-stepped his chair, and pushed it under the table. "Pain in the ass fixin' cars in the parking lot, I'll tell ya. Be nice when that new garage is finished."

"Glad to see Lenny decided to rebuild the garage after the fire," Sam said.

"Me too," Artie agreed. "I'm gettin' way too old to look for another job."

"When's he think the new garage will be completed?" Ben asked.

"The contractor says he'll be done by the end of July," Artie answered. He turned and made his way across the old oak floor to the front of the restaurant. "See ya later," he grumbled, pushed open the door, and disappeared into the darkness.

"Another hand?" Curt asked as he shuffled the deck.

John looked at his watch. "Yeah, what the hell."

Sam stood. "Another round of drinks?"

"Yeah, what the hell," said Ben.

Sam walked around behind the bar and made himself a Black Velvet and ginger ale. For Curt he drew a pint of Guinness from the tap. He made John a rum and Coke, and for Ben he poured a shot of Scotch over ice in a short glass. He placed the four drinks on a small round tray and delivered them to the table. When Sam set Curt's beer in front of him, Curt smacked him on the ass.

"Prettiest waitress in town," Curt joked.

"I bet you say that to all the boys," Sam shot back.

"I only have eyes for you, baby," Curt replied.

"Just deal," John scolded. "Christ, I should just stay home and play board games with Jenny and the kids. They're a little less annoying."

Curt dealt each man five cards. "Deuces and one-eyed jacks are wild."

After a few more hands John Morgan decided that he'd better head on home, and the rest of the men agreed.

Curt counted his chips and announced that he was the big winner of the night, being eight dollars ahead. He traded in his chips and went out the door.

"You need help picking up here?" Ben asked Sam.

"No," Sam replied. "I'll just have Marcia clean up in the morning."

"I bet that'll make her happy," said John.

"You walking home, John?" Ben asked.

"Yeah, I think so. Nice night for a walk."

Sam said his good byes and went into the kitchen to turn out the lights and shut off the deep fryer. John and

Ben walked out the front door and onto sidewalk, and let the door close behind them.

Ben looked up Main Street to his left and then to his right toward the ocean. He took a deep breath and slowly exhaled. "I'll never get sick of that salty ocean air," he said.

"I know what you mean," John agreed. He took a deep breath as well. He pulled his lighter from his front pocket and relit his stub of a cigar. "I grew up in Detroit, and looking back I can't imagine why *anyone* would live in a big city. Nope, small town life, that's the life for me."

"When did you settle here?" Ben asked.

"June of '89. Got a job at the grocery store as a stock boy a couple months later."

"And with a lot of hard work, now you own the place. The American dream fulfilled."

The giant of a man laughed. "I guess there was some hard work involved, but marrying the owner's daughter didn't hurt."

The two men turned and started up Main Street. They passed the Grape Vine Wine Shoppe, and Olsen's Candy Store, and when they were directly across the street from Dunquin Pharmacy, John asked, "Did you see that?"

"See what?" Ben asked.

"Thought I saw a light in the drug store."

"I don't see anything."

They walked a few more steps and John froze, saying, "There it is again. It looks like a flashlight."

"Yeah, I saw it that time," said Ben.

"You think it's Cecil?"

"I think Cecil would have turned on the lights."

The two men started across the street toward the pharmacy.

"Should we call the cops?" John asked.

"Let's see what's going on first."

Ben walked up and put his back against the wall on one side of the door and John did the same on the other. Both men craned their necks around and looked through the glass door at the same time. They watched for a moment until they saw a dark shadow pass by the end of one of the aisles. The figure was carrying a flashlight in one hand and a large bag in the other. They quickly pulled their heads back.

"Who do you think it is?" John asked.

"Definitely not Cecil," Ben answered. "Unless Cecil grew five inches since yesterday."

"Yeah, and gained forty pounds. Should we call the cops?"

Ben grinned. "We probably should, but wouldn't it be more fun to take care of it ourselves?"

John shook his head. "What is it with you and this *taking matters into your own hands* thing you seem to love so much?"

"I really don't know." Ben crouched down and quietly pulled open the door. He duck walked through the door, with John right behind him, and made a quick right, moving behind the checkout counter.

They could hear a voice and John whispered, "Either he's talking to himself of there's more than one of them."

"Sounds like it came from back by the pharmacy counter," Ben whispered back.

"I wish I had a gun."

"Well, let's go get a couple." As they crawled out from behind the register and headed down one of the aisles, they could hear two men arguing at the back of the store. One man was telling the other to quit making so much noise, while the other man kept insisting, "You're not the boss of me."

When Ben and John got to the toy aisle Ben reached up and grabbed two squirt guns and removed them from their packages.

"Did you hear that?" one of the unknown men asked.

"You're imagining things," the other man told him.

Ben handed one of the pistols to John.

"I meant that I wished I had a real gun," John informed him.

"They're as real as the bad guys think they are."

Ben and John got to their feet and tip-toed to the end of the aisle and watched the thugs from behind an end cap filled with Fig Newtons. The larger of the two criminals held the flashlight as the other one filled a plastic kitchen garbage bag with prescription bottles and large clear bags filled with pills.

"Good enough," the larger man said. "Let's get out of here."

They both back turned and walked through the door that separated the pharmacy from the rest of the store. As they exited they came face to face with Ben and John, and their plastic arsenal.

"Did you gentleman find everything okay?" John asked.

The two men froze in their tracks. "Shit!" the smaller one said.

"Drop that bag," Ben ordered. "And walk toward the front of the store. One wrong move and I blow your goddamn head off."

The little guy didn't move. "We need these drugs," he said. "Snake is waiting for us."

"Snake, who's Snake?" John asked.

A deep voice behind them said, "*I'm* Snake. Now drop those guns before I blow *your* goddamn heads off."

The man with the flashlight shined it on Ben and John. "Hey, those aren't even real guns," he said.

Both men let go of their squirt guns at the same time and put up their hands. The plastic pistols hit the floor with a crack.

Snake threw back his head and laughed. "They're squirt guns! What kind of an asshole tries to stop a robbery with a squirt gun?"

"I guess that would be us," Ben said.

"Shut up!" Snake ordered. "Donny, grab some duct tape. Jack keep the flash light on them."

Donny handed the pillowcase to Jack and ran directly to the duct tape.

"I knew that kid looked familiar," John said. "That's Donny Reilly; he used to work here. His father owns the feed store out on Route Four."

"Shit," Donny said when he returned with the tape. "They know who I am. What are we gonna do?"

"Well, Donny, I guess that means we'll either have to kill them, or you," Snake responded.

"You said no one would get hurt, Snake," Donny pleaded.

"Just tape up their hands; we'll put them in the trunk and bring them with us."

Keeping the roll in his left hand, Donny picked at the end of the tape with his fingernail. When he had loosened a corner he unrolled about two feet of the gray tape and moved toward Ben.

Ben put his wrists together and when Donny had closed the distance between them, Ben thrust his right hand through the roll of duct tape and in one lightning-quick movement wrapped the tape around Donny's wrists.

Donny's eyes widened as Ben grabbed him by the hands and swung him around, smashing him into Snake.

As Snake lost his balance he fired his weapon once, the bullet lodging in the center of Jack's brain. Jack's head snapped back; he hit the tile floor as lifeless as the bag of stolen medication he was holding.

Ben released his grip on Donny and the two thugs hit the pharmacy counter together. The side of Snake's head struck the edge of the Formica counter, knocking him out cold, his weapon flying from his hand and skidding across the floor.

Donny lay on his side, on top of Snake, looking up at Ben.

John dropped to his knees and recovered Snakes pistol. "Wow!" he exclaimed admiringly. "What the hell was that?"

Ben held out his hand and John placed the weapon in his palm. "Probably karate or judo or something. Who knows?"

"You gotta teach me to do that."

"I don't even know who taught *me* to do that." Ben aimed the 9mm at Donny. "Get up!"

Donny obeyed instantly.

Ben grabbed the front of Donny's shirt and yanked him over closer to Jack's body. Donny turned his head away. "Look at him!" Ben shouted. "That could just as easily be your blood spilling out all over the floor."

Tears were streaming down Donny's cheeks. "Please don't kill me."

Ben put his face close to Donny's. "Consider this the most important day in your life." Ben shoved the kid away. "Get home. Now."

"How?"

"Run."

"It's fifteen miles."

"It's better than fifteen years, stupid. Now get going."

Donny turned and ran for the front door.

"You're just going to let him go?" John asked.

"Why, you think that boy will ever commit another crime?"

John laughed. "I wouldn't think so."

Both men looked over as Snake groaned and started coming around. He sat up.

"You okay?" Ben asked.

"I ... I think so." Snake felt the side of his head and then stared at the blood on his hand. "I'm bleeding."

"Aw, that's too bad," Ben said. He crouched down, grabbed the back of Snakes head, and shoved the 9mm up under the thug's chin. "You're going to prison for a long time, Snake. Not because of the theft, but for the murder of your little friend over there."

John stepped aside so Snake could get a good look at Jack.

"Oh shit," Snake said. "Where's Donny?"

Ben pushed harder with the gun and Snake tensed.

"Donny wasn't here tonight," Ben said. "It was only you and Jack."

"But—"

"But nothing." Ben moved closer. "You've seen what I can do. If you ever mention Donny's name, I'll find you and I'll kill you. It doesn't matter where you are. Do you understand?"

Ben was now pushing the barrel of the gun so forcefully into Snake's chin that he couldn't answer.

Ben pulled back the hammer of the gun and asked again, calmly: "I said, do you understand."

As best he could Snake slowly nodded his head yes.

"Good," Ben said gleefully. He searched the floor near him. "Where's the duct tape?"

"Donny was still wearing it when he ran out the door," John replied.

"Oh." Ben raised the gun in the air and brought the grip down on top of Snakes head. Snake slumped over and his head hit the floor. "There, he's not going anywhere." Ben handed the weapon to John. "You call the cops. I'm going home."

John took the gun. "What do you mean, you're going home?"

"John, you know I can't have my name or picture in the paper."

"Fine. Get out of here."

Ben walked out the door and John glanced over at the unconscious Snake and said, "Don't go anywhere asshole, I gotta make a phone call."

Chapter Two

"Come on, Mica!" Clair shouted up the stairs. "The bus will be here any second."

"I'm coming," the ten-year-old shouted back. The young boy was searching his room frantically for his other sneaker.

Ben sat at the dining room table reading the morning edition of the *Duncan Crier* and drinking a cup of coffee. He could see Claire at the end of the hall near the bottom of the stairs as she waited patiently. She was holding Mica's book bag in one hand and a blueberry muffin in the other.

The front door was standing open. Ben watched the old yellow school bus pull up in front of the house. The strident squeal of its brakes made his skin crawl. The door swung open, and Ben saw the driver scowl toward the house. Having to wait for Mica happened much too often.

"Mica, the bus is here. Let's go!" Claire yelled.

She ran out on the front porch and hollered "he's coming!" The driver gave a half-smile and a half-heartedly raised a finger from the wheel in greeting. He checked his wristwatch pointedly.

As Ben sipped his coffee he heard Mica run down the upstairs hall and then down the stairs. When the boy reached the bottom of the stairs he grabbed his book bag and the muffin, ran out onto the porch, and jumped over the steps to the ground. Neither sneaker was tied.

"Don't trip over those laces!" Claire yelled, but Mica was already on the bus and the door was closing. She pulled the screen door shut and watched as the bus pulled away from the curb and lurched down the street with a rickety whine.

"Mornings seem to be getting louder around here," Ben commented, as Claire walked back through the dining room and into the kitchen.

"I don't know what it is with that boy," Claire grumbled. "It takes forever to get him out of bed in the morning, and then he waits till the last minute to get dressed."

Ben kept reading the paper as Claire rambled on in the kitchen. Every once in a while he would let out an "uh-huh," just so she thought he was listening.

The phone rang and Claire answered, "Colsome House Bed and Breakfast, Claire speaking. How can I help you? Oh, hello, Jenny … I'm not sure … He didn't mention anything."

Ben turned his ear toward the kitchen door. He knew he was probably the *he* in *he didn't mention anything.*

"That's crazy," Claire gasped. "I can't believe it." There was a long pause as Claire listened to Jenny, and then she said, "Okay, Jenny, I'll talk to you later."

Ben picked up his paper and began reading again.

Claire walked into the dining room. "That was Jenny Morgan," she said. "She was telling me that John stopped a robbery last night at the pharmacy."

"Wow! Really?"

"Yeah. She said he saw someone inside the store as he walked by."

"That's crazy."

"That's what I said. She said he fought with the two guys and one of them was shot and killed."

"Well, that's really something. I'm sure he'll call me later today to brag about what a hero he is."

"He's lucky he wasn't killed."

"I'll say."

Claire stared at Ben for a second. "You don't seem very surprised. What time did you come in last night?"

"Eleven thirty, I believe."

"What time did John leave the Cove?"

"I don't know. He must have left after me." Ben picked up his mug to take another sip of his coffee. The cup was empty so he stood and went into the kitchen to refill it.

Claire followed him into the kitchen. "The whole thing sounds more like something you would do, not John Morgan. John's a big guy, but he's more the gentle giant type."

"A regular teddy bear," Ben agreed. He poured his coffee. "Well, maybe I've just been a good influence on the guy."

"Yeah, maybe," Claire agreed. "Wait, *good* influence?"

Ben set his cup on the counter, put his arms around Claire, and kissed her on the forehead. "Just be glad he walked by when he did. That's two more bad guys off the street."

"I guess," said Claire. She put her head on Ben's shoulder. "You hungry?" she asked.

"Yes."

"You want me to make you something?"

"Why don't you grab a cup of coffee, go sit down and read the paper, and I'll make *you* breakfast."

"That sounds even better," Claire responded.

*****

After breakfast Ben cleared the table and loaded the dishes into the dish washer. "I think I'll head over to the store and talk to John," he said.

Claire folded the newspaper and placed it to the side. "Can you pick up a few things for me?" she asked.

"Sure. You have a list made up?"

"I'll make one quick." Claire got up from the table and went into the kitchen.

Ben went into the living room to put on his shoes and when he returned to the dining room Claire handed him the list.

"Here ya go," she said.

Ben read the list aloud. "Milk, bread, dish detergent, coffee, something for dinner." He looked at Claire. "Something for dinner?" he asked.

"Just grab something to throw on the grill."

"Like what?"

"Whatever you want."

"Okay," Ben said. He folded the list and stuck it in his back pocket. They kissed and Ben went out the door.

No sooner did Claire hear Ben's truck start and pull away from the house than the phone rang.

"Colsome House Bed and Breakfast, Claire speaking. How may I help you?"

A deep voice with a slight Boston accent said "Good morning, Claire. I was wondering if you could help me."

"I'll try," Claire offered.

"I'm looking for a friend of mine and I heard he might be staying at your establishment."

"We don't have any guests at the moment. Can you give me your friend's name?"

"His name is Max Wright." There was a pause. "Does that name sound familiar to you?"

"The name doesn't ring a bell, but I can check my guest registry. We don't usually give out information about our guests, but if he has stayed here and I have his number, I can have him contact you."

"That would be fantastic, Claire."

Claire picked up the pen that lay next to the phone. "Can I have your name and number please?"

"My name is Flannigan ... Neal Flannigan."

"And may I have your number?"

"Certainly. It's 617-555-0138."

Claire jotted down the number and laid the pen on the pad of paper. "Okay, Mr. Flannigan, I'll try to get that information, if I have it. If that name doesn't come up in my guest log would you like me to call you back and let you know?"

"No, that's quite all right, Claire. I'm sure Max will be calling me back shortly."

"Uh, okay. Well, you have a nice day, Mr. Flannigan."

"And you as well, Claire. Thank you."

Chapter Three

Ben pulled his truck to the curb in front of Lita's Bakery and walked across the street to the grocery store. As he approached the meat counter, at the back of the store, he heard an elderly woman say, "My goodness, John, you could have been hurt, or even killed. You should have just called the police."

"Well, there wasn't really time for that," John answered.

"You're a real hero, John," the old woman said.

"I'm no hero," John argued. "I just did what any other man would do if put in that situation. I saw those guys in the drug store and my first thought was the good people of Dunquin—"

"Oh, come on," Ben interrupted. "Don't be so modest. You're a hero all right."

John shot his friend a warning look.

"No, I mean it," Ben insisted. "We should see if the mayor will give you the key to the village."

John laughed uncomfortably.

"Maybe he's right." she said seriously. "Good Samaritans should be rewarded."

"How are you today Mrs. Penobscot?" Ben asked the old woman.

"Oh, I guess any day you wake up on this side of the grass is a good one. How's Claire and Mica? That boy is getting so big. I remember the day he was born; snow coming down like—"

"Here ya go, Mrs. Penobscot," John said, handing her a package of bologna.

"They're good," Ben answered.

Mrs. Penobscot placed the package of meat into her shopping cart with the rest of her groceries and said, "Well, I better get going. Myron will be wondering where his lunch is. If I died tomorrow that man would starve to death in three days." As she pushed the cart down the aisle the front wheel wobbled and let out a squeal with each rotation.

"Might be time for some new shopping carts," Ben pointed out. "Looks like that one was around when Christ shopped here."

"I think Mrs. Penobscot shopped here then too," John remarked.

"Sounds like you're the town hero."

"Yeah, thanks for that. Jenny was pretty pissed off when she found out."

"What did Chet say?"

"He was pretty pissed too. He said I should have called the cops instead of handling it myself."

"He's only saying that because he's the chief of police. He's just bored and wanted something to bitch about. Cecil must have been grateful."

"He was, but he did mention the display of Fig Newtons you crushed. I think he wanted me to pay for them."

"Yeah, collateral damage will get you every time."

"I guess," John replied. "So, did you come in here just to bust my balls or did you need something?"

Ben removed the list from his back pocket. "I need something for dinner."

"Something for dinner, aye." John scanned the display cooler. "How about a few of these pork chops?"

Ben turned up his nose. "Naw."

"Chicken?"

"Just give me three of those Delmonico steaks."

"Comin' right up," John said, as he slid the cooler door open. He grabbed three of the steaks and tossed them on the scales. "That good?"

Ben glanced at the digital read out. "Looks good to me. Your thumb's not on that scale, is it?"

"Slightly." John tore a piece of butcher's paper from the roll that sat on the counter behind him. "Raining out there yet?" he asked.

"Not yet, but it looks like it could start at any minute."

John taped up the package, stuck the price tag on the side, and handed it over the counter to Ben. "The weekend is supposed to be pretty nice."

"That's what they're saying. So long, hero man."

"So long, jackhole."

Ben walked around the store picking up the remaining items on the list. He checked out and lugged his grocery bags across the street toward his red and white 1994 Ford F-150. As he walked along he thought about the conversation he had just had with his friend John about the weather. He wondered if he had those same meaningless conversations in his old life, and if he did, who he had them with.

Ben Dunning had come to Dunquin Cove, Maine, a little less than a year ago, after an automobile accident left him with no memory of his past. Ben Dunning was the name Claire gave him the day after he stumbled up the street and collapsed in the front yard of the Colsome House Bed and Breakfast. She told everyone in town that Ben was her deceased husband's brother. Over the next few days, Claire—the owner of the B&B—nursed him back to health. In the months that followed Ben tried his best to solve the mystery of his true identity through clues and information acquired from some of Boston's most disreputable citizens.

So far Ben had learned that he had lived for years under the name Wesley Hargreaves in Medford, Massachusetts. He had a home there and was good friends with his neighbors, who thought he worked in real estate. Ben had discovered one extremely disturbing fact: his real name was Max Wright, and he was a freelance hit man.

"Snap out of it, handsome," Lita Tanner said, snapping her fingers twice above her head. "You look like you're a million miles away."

Ben looked across the hood of his truck to see the plump brunette sitting on the bench in front of the bakery she operated with her husband Howard. "Good morning, Lita," Ben called out. "I was just wondering if I should get an apple pie or a cherry pie for dessert."

Lita cackled. "I can make that choice a little easier for ya."

"You can, can you?"

"Yup. Were fresh out of cherry pie."

Ben opened his truck door and placed his two bags of groceries on the seat. "Well, I guess it'll be apple then." He slammed the truck door and walked around to the sidewalk.

"Fresh coffee inside," Lita said, lifting the half-empty mug she was holding.

"That actually sounds pretty good."

"You go right in and help yourself. Howard should be stumbling around in there somewhere."

Ben walked up the steps and through the door.

Lita and Howard had set up a small table next to the door upon which sat a coffee maker, creamers, and packets of sugar. Ben picked up one of the mugs that sat next to the Mr. Coffee and poured himself a cup. The sound of metal baking trays clanging together told Ben that Howard was busy in the kitchen, so he returned to the bench out front and took a seat next to Lita. Lita's large behind left less than half the bench for Ben to sit, and in the back of his mind there was a tiny fear that the old wooden slats wouldn't hold both of them. He sat down with caution, trying his best not to make Lita aware of his fears.

Lita and her skinny-as-a-rail husband, Howard, were the original owners of Lita's Bakery, opening the shop in the late seventies. The couple, who were now in their mid-sixties, showed no signs of retirement or slowing down.

"You hear what happened over to the drugstore last night?" Lita asked, nodding her head in that direction.

"John just told me about it," Ben answered.

"That was really something the way he apprehended the thieves. Did you know John knew karate?"

"I had no idea," Ben replied. "Did John tell you that?"

"No, I haven't spoken to him yet. I guess he told Curt, and Curt told Sam, and Sam told me."

"The old small town-a-graph."

Lita chuckled. "That's how the word spreads. I guess they both had guns, but John was able to disarm them."

"Both of them?"

"Yup."

"Incredible."

"I think I'll give him a free pie for his family's desert tonight. Just to show our appreciation. We're lucky to have a man like that living in this town."

"We sure are," Ben agreed. He downed the remainder of his coffee and stood up.

"Here, I'll take that cup," Lita said, reaching out for it.

"I'll bring it in," Ben insisted. "I wanted to grab something any way."

Ben walked back up the steps and Lita followed. He walked up to the glass bakery case and Lita walked around behind it. "What can I get for you?" she asked.

"I'll take a half dozen of those half-moon cookies and—hey, I thought you said you were out of cherry pie? There's one sitting right there."

Lita made an apologetic face and sucked air through her clenched teeth. "That's the one I was gonna give to John."

"I'll take the *apple* pie," Ben groaned.

Chapter Four

Ben placed the apple pie and half-moon cookies on the counter top and the steaks in the refrigerator.

"What did you get to go with the steaks?" Claire asked as rummaging through the two grocery bags.

"Potatoes," Ben answered. "And corn on the cob."

Claire pulled out a clear plastic bag that contained four large potatoes. "Who's the fourth one for?" she asked.

Ben shrugged. "Better to have one too many than be one short."

"True. How would you like me to cook them?"

"With heat," Ben replied.

"Smart ass. Baked or mashed?"

"Baked."

As the couple put the remainder of the groceries away, Claire asked, "So, did John tell you any more about what happened last night?"

"Three guys tried to rob the drug store and John stopped them."

Claire cocked her head. "Jenny said it was only two guys."

"Oh. Maybe it was. Maybe he did say two. I wasn't really paying attention."

Claire walked over and put her arms around Ben and gave him a sad little smile. "Sounds like someone might be just a little bit jealous that John is getting all this attention."

Ben kissed her on the forehead. "Don't be ridiculous," he said.

Claire turned and opened the white bakery box. "Half-moons. Mica's going to like that." She glanced at the pie. "How come you didn't get a cherry pie?"

Ben shook his head. "Lita was saving that for the new town hero," he answered disgustedly.

Claire laughed so hard that she snorted.

"Yeah, laugh it up," said Ben.

The clothes dryer buzzer sounded. "It's playing my tune," she announced.

As she walked by on her way to the cellar door, Ben slapped her on the ass. "Get those chores done, woman," he said jokingly.

On her way down the cellar stairs she hollered up, "Hey, you remember a guy staying here by the name of Max Wright?"

Ben froze. "Who?" he shouted back. He walked to the top of the cellar stairs and listened for Claire's response.

"A guy named Max Wright," she repeated.

Ben swallowed hard. "Doesn't sound familiar. Why do you ask?"

"Hold on," Claire hollered. "I'll be back up in a second."

Ben turned, opened the refrigerator, and grabbed a pitcher full of iced tea. He poured himself a glass and drank half of it in the first gulp.

Claire walked back into the kitchen carrying a basket of freshly dried laundry. "Yeah, someone called here right after you left looking for a man named Max Wright."

Ben returned the pitcher to the refrigerator and shut the door. "What did you tell him?"

"I told him the name didn't sound familiar, but I would look in the guest registry and see if it was in there."

"He leave his name?"

"Yeah. I wrote it down with his number. It's next to the phone."

"Are you supposed to call him back?"

"No, he said that even if I didn't find the name he was expecting a call from the guy any way."

Claire left the kitchen and headed upstairs. Ben waited until he was sure she was in their bedroom and hurried to the phone. He read the name on the note pad: Neal Flannigan.

Who the hell is Neil Flannigan? Ben wondered. *And why is he looking for Max Wright?* He tore a page out of the pad, copied down the phone number, and shoved it into his pocket.

Knock, knock!

Ben turned to see a familiar silhouette in the front door's glass panel. He sidestepped to the door, turned the knob, and pulled it open.

"Good morning, Marvin," Ben greeted.

"Morning?" the old man replied. "It's almost the afternoon. What time are we getting started on that garage door?"

"*We*?" Ben asked.

"You didn't think I was gonna make you tackle that project on your own, did ya? What kind of neighbor would I be if I didn't come over here and give you a hand?"

"The perfect kind," Ben grumbled to himself.

"What's that?" Marvin asked.

"Nothing." Ben stepped back away from the door and motioned for Marvin to enter. "Cup of coffee?"

"Sounds good," the eighty-year-old answered as he bent down to pick up an old wooden toolbox.

"What do you have there?"

"My tools. I always come prepared." Marvin stepped inside. "My boy, Jack, built me this tool box when he was in school. That boy was always good with his hands. Not real good with his head—God rest his soul—but the boy could build anything."

"We could sure use him today then, because I sure as hell don't know anything about installing a new garage door." Ben shut the front door and started back down the hall toward the dining room.

"Nonsense," Marvin said. "You have nothing to worry about. I'll be right there with you every step of the way."

Lucky me, Ben thought.

Ben made Marvin a cup of coffee, and the two men carried their cups out to the garage to have a look at the rotted old overhead door. They stood side by side sipping their coffee and staring at the door.

"Where should we start?" Ben asked.

"Where's the new door?" Marvin asked.

"In the garage … still in the box," Ben replied.

Marvin scratched his head. "Hmm," he said. "I guess the first thing we should do is tear out the old door."

"You ever install one of these before?"

"No, but how hard could it be?"

"Famous last words." Ben walked to the door and tried to lift it with one hand. "It's stuck again."

"I'll go around to the side," Marvin offered. He went to the wooden door on the side of the garage and let himself in. Ben waited a few seconds and then heard Marvin shout, "Here's the problem."

"What's the matter?" Ben called out.

"Spring's broken."

"Do new springs come with the new door?"

"I would think so. You'll have to come in here. Probably be easier to remove this thing from the inside."

Ben walked around and entered through the side door.

Marvin pointed at the broken spring hanging from its safety line. "See there, broken spring."

Ben stared at the dangling piece of coiled metal. "Common sense says we should lift the door to take the tension off the other spring before we remove it," he said, nodding his head sagely

"Common sense? Never heard of it," Marvin joked, and went to the back of the garage to retrieve a six-foot step ladder. He placed the ladder under the good spring and returned to the rear of the garage to grab an old pair of tin snips lying on the work bench.

"What are you doing there?" Ben asked.

"You'll see."

Marvin climbed to the second step of the ladder, reached up, and clipped the safety line. Nothing happened. Then he clipped the tension line sending the spring flying to the back wall of the garage and through the rear window shattering the glass.

Both men walked to the window and stared out at the spring that was now lying half way across the backyard.

"Lot of tension on those springs," Ben pointed out.

"Yeah," Marvin agreed. "Probably gonna want to take this window sash over to Cargill's Hardware and have Dave put a new piece of glass in her."

Ben and Marvin still had their coffee mugs in their hands. "Another cup of coffee?" Ben asked.

"Good idea," said Marvin. "We don't want to move on to step two with an empty mug."

"Step one being spring removal?"

"Yup."

"What step was breaking the window?"

"Step one-B, wise ass."

The duo left the garage and headed toward the back door.

"What the hell is all the racket over here?" Alan Cobb asked, as he walked around the back of the B&B toward the DIY'ers.

Alan Cobb was Marvin and Ben's across-the-street neighbor. He was a few years younger than Marvin, but still quite a few years older than Ben. Alan was retired military. He had a crew-cut, was clean shaven, and had grown a large belly in the thirty years or so since retirement. Ben had always wondered if Alan's bow legs were from birth or a symptom of downward force from his large gut. Alan wore blue jeans with the pant legs tucked into his black military style boots, a white wife beater, and an unbuttoned, long-sleeved flannel shirt.

"Putting in a new garage door," Marvin informed him.

"Sounded like glass breaking," said Cobb.

"Yeah, we heard that too," Ben said.

"Came from down the street," Marvin added.

Cobb shrugged. "Got one of those cups for me?" he asked.

"Come on," Ben replied, and led the two men through the back door and up the four steps into the kitchen. He grabbed another mug out of the cupboard for Cobb and filled it with coffee. He filled Marvin's cup too, and then his own.

Ben paused when he heard Claire's voice coming from the hall so he stepped into the kitchen doorway to listen.

"You're welcome, Mr. Flannigan," Claire said into the phone. Okay, goodbye. You have a wonderful day." She hung up the phone, turned toward the dining room, and saw Ben watching her.

"You called him back?" Ben asked.

"Yes. I wanted to let him know that his friend Max Wright had never stayed here."

"Did he believe you?"

Claire cocked her head. "Yes," she replied. "Why wouldn't he believe me?"

"Who?" Marvin asked.

Ben ignored him. "No, I just mean that he was so sure that his friend stayed here. Maybe he thought you were mistaken."

"Who?" Marvin persisted.

"I gave him the names of a few other B&Bs in the area. He said he would check them out."

"Who?" Marvin inquired once again.

Cobb rolled his eyes. "Jesus Christ, Marvin, you shit through branches too?" he asked.

"Let me know if he calls back," Ben said.

"Shit through branches?" Marvin asked.

"Yeah," Cobb said. "You sound like a damn owl. Who, who, who?"

"Up yours, Cobb," Marvin responded. "I was invited over here. You, on the other hand, came uninvited."

Ben put up his hand to shush them both. "Both of you be quiet for a second." He turned back to Claire, but she had already gone up the stairs.

"See," Cobb said. "You got us both yelled at."

"But mostly you," said Marvin.

Ben rolled his eyes. "Come on, let's get back out there and get that door in."

"Good idea," Marvin said.

"Ass kisser," Cobb said quietly, and then made a smooching sound with his lips.

Ben led the way back out the door and to the garage, all the while wondering if he had heard the last of Neil Flannigan.

Chapter Five

At five thirty the following morning the alarm clock lit up and the radio began playing Jefferson Airplane's "White Rabbit." Ben rolled over onto his back and rubbed his eyes as Grace Slick sang the last few lines of the song in her signature full-throated vibrato.

Now the cheesy disc jockey was saying, "Good morning, sleepy heads! I'm Big Larry Lincoln, and this is 104.2 the greatest radio station in Dunquin Cove, because it's the only radio station in Dunquin Cove."

Ben rolled his eyes and turned his head toward the bedroom window; it was still dark outside. He swung his legs over the edge of the bed and walked across the room to the alarm clock on a mission to silence Big Larry Lincoln.

It was Claire's idea to put the alarm clock on the chest of drawers on the other side of the bedroom. Her thinking was that if you had to get out of bed to shut it off, there was a greater chance you wouldn't hit snooze and fall back asleep. Ben never understood this since Claire was always out of bed, dressed, and downstairs before the alarm sounded any way.

Ben flipped on the wall switch and blinked as the room flooded with light. He turned to see himself in the full-length mirror across the room. He stood inspecting himself dressed in just his boxers. *I'm getting flabby*, he thought, and poked at his belly with his index finger. *Retired hit men should be in much better shape*.

As Ben walked down the stairs he could smell bacon cooking. *Too many home cooked meals, that's probably why I'm out of shape,* he mused.

"Good morning," Claire said as Ben entered the kitchen. She stood in front of the stove in her white and black cow print pajamas, turning over each piece of bacon one at a time.

"Morning," Ben returned.

Claire glanced down at Ben's feet. "Why are you wearing sneakers?" she asked.

Ben shrugged and then reached into the cupboard for a coffee mug. "I was thinking about going for a run."

"A run? You don't run."

Ben filled his cup. "Maybe I do. How would I know?" Ben figured his body would remind him during the run whether it was something he had done before or not.

"I guess you have a point there," Claire agreed.

Ben blew into the hot coffee and then took a small sip to test the temperature. "I was just going to try a mile and see how I did."

Claire turned and peered through the window above the sink that looked out over the backyard. "Are you going to wait until it gets light out?"

"No. I don't want anyone to see me."

"If they don't see you, they won't be able to find you in the street to administer CPR."

"Thanks for the vote of confidence." Ben kissed her on the cheek, spun around, and headed for the front door.

Ben made his way down the walkway and onto the sidewalk. He stood for a minute and looked north up Shore Drive and then turned his head in the other direction. He glanced across the street; the Cobbs' lights were on. He turned and looked back at Marvin's place; his lights were on as well. Old people get up early.

Here goes nothing, Ben thought and began jogging up Shore Drive toward downtown. At first his gait felt clumsy and foreign, but by the time he reached Felton Street his breathing slowed and synchronized with the movement of his arms and legs; he was sure he had done this many times before.

Ben made it to the street light at the corner of Main and Shore and took a left. He ran past the White Rose Diner and Farmwell's Department Store on his left. He looked to his right and surveyed the recent construction at Lenny's Garage. He took a right on Lake Street, and then a right onto Denton Street, and ran past Cargill's Hardware Store. He remembered the broken window he needed to get repaired. Then Ben hung a right back onto Shore Drive and headed for home. When he crossed Main Street he looked back over his shoulder at the grocery store; John Morgan was unlocking the front door. John turned his head when he heard the patter of sneakers on the pavement and watched the runner in the darkness, wondering who it was. Ben quickly looked in the other direction so as not to be recognized.

Ben slowed to a walk when he reached the opening in the wrought iron fence that ran around the front yard of the Colsome House Bed and Breakfast. He walked to the end of the block, turned around, and returned to the house.

"How did it go?" Claire called out from the kitchen when she heard the front door shut.

Ben tossed the morning edition of the *Dunquin Crier* on the dining room table on his way to the kitchen. "Good," he replied.

"You're not even sweating," Claire observed.

"I guess I'm not in as bad a shape as I thought I was." Ben picked up his half full coffee mug from earlier, placed it in the microwave, and set the timer for forty-five seconds.

"How far did you go?" Claire asked

"One point two miles."

Claire looked at him with one eyebrow raised. "One point two miles?" she asked with a slight chuckle. "Exactly?"

"Pretty damn close."

"And how would you know that?"

The microwave dinged and Ben grabbed his cup. "I guess the same way I seemed to know that I was running at a seven-minute, twenty-eight second pace and my heart rate was 175 when I finished." He took a big gulp of his coffee.

"Oh," Claire said suspiciously. She glanced up at the wall clock. "I better wake up Mica."

"I'll wake him up," Ben said. He turned and walked out of the kitchen.

Claire watched him as he made his way through the dining room and down the hall toward the staircase, wondering what he would be remembering next. There had always been a fear inside her that Ben would leave someday when his memories completely returned.

Just as Ben reached the top step and rounded the newel post, the phone rang; Claire went to answer it, and he proceeded to Mica's room.

"Colsome House Bed and Breakfast," Claire said into the phone. "How may I help you?" She paused to wait for an answer, but none came. "Hello?" she said again. Claire listened closely and could hear the faint sound of someone breathing. "Hello?" She shrugged and returned the phone to its cradle.

"Who was that?" Ben asked as he descended the stairs.

"They didn't say anything," Claire responded. "Must have been a wrong number."

"Yeah, maybe," Ben replied. *Or maybe not*, he thought.

"Is Mica up?"

"He's awake, but moving slowly."

"I don't want him to miss the school bus again."

"I already told him I would give him a ride to school. I have to go to the hardware store this morning for something anyway."

"The older he gets, the harder it is to get him out of bed in the morning. Were you that way when you—oh, sorry."

Ben smiled. "I would imagine I was the same way."

The phone rang again, this time Ben picked it up. "Hello?" he said. There was a long pause and then Ben said "hello" again.

"Is this Max Wright?" a man asked.

"I think you have the wrong number," Ben replied.

"Do I?"

"Yes, you definitely do." Ben hung up the phone. "You're right, it was a wrong number."

After breakfast Ben and Mica walked out the back door and to the garage.

"The new door looks great," Mica said. "You guys did a really good job."

"How much?" Ben asked.

"How much? How much what?"

"The new door looks great. You guys did a really good job," Ben aped. "I figure you must be buttering me up for something."

"No," Mica replied.

Ben grabbed hold of the door handle and lifted. The door rose with ease to about the halfway point, made a loud clunk, and then stopped dead. "Dammit!"

"What's the matter?" Mica asked.

"Who knows? We'll take my truck."

Chapter Six

After dropping Mica off in front of the school Ben made a U-turn on Maple Street, took a quick left onto Denton Street, and parked in front of Cargill's Hardware.

"Morning, Dave," Ben said as he entered the store.

Dave Cargill looked up from the register and smiled. "Morning, Ben. How are you today?"

"Good, Dave. You?"

"Can't complain. Nobody would listen if I did. What can I do for you?"

Ben reached into his pocket and pulled out a folded piece of paper. "I need a piece of glass."

"You got the size there?" Dave reached for the paper.

"Yeah."

Dave walked around the counter. "Let's go back in the stockroom and see what we got."

Ben and Dave walked to the back of the store and through a door that said EMPLOYEES ONLY.

"You hear about John Morgan stopping those thieves over at the drugstore the other night?" Dave asked as he looked through pieces of glass that stood on end in a wooden rack.

"Several times," Ben remarked.

"Ha-ha. Yeah, I bet. Just about everyone who's come in here in the last two days has mentioned it. Did you see this morning's paper?"

"Threw it on the table and never opened it. Why, what's in there?"

"Big write-up on the front page, along with John's photograph."

Ben rolled his eyes. "Oh, brother. I guess this is his fifteen minutes of fame."

"Here we go," said Dave as he pulled a sheet of glass out of the rack. "This should do it."

Dave laid the glass on a felt-covered table and used a hand-held glass cutter to cut the glass into the exact measurements that Ben needed. When he was finished he wrapped the glass in brown paper and taped down the folds with masking tape. "Can I get you anything else?"

"Yeah. You got some of that putty stuff you put around the glass?"

"Glazing compound," Dave informed him.

"Yeah, that stuff."

Dave picked up the glass and said, "Follow me." The two men walked out of the stockroom and down one of the aisles. Dave picked up a small can of glazing compound and handed it to Ben. "Anything else?"

"I don't think so," Ben replied.

"You got a putty knife?"

"So, you use a putty knife, but it's not called putty?"

"Yup."

"I think I have a putty knife."

"Okey doke. Let's get you rung up."

Ben carefully laid the pane of glass in the bed of his truck and tossed the can of glazing on the front seat. As he pulled away from the curb he decided to visit John Morgan at the grocery store. He pulled to the curb on Shore Drive and parked under a massive red maple, and then walked around the corner to the grocery store. As he pulled open the door he glanced back over his shoulder at a man who was sitting on the bench in front of the bakery drinking a cup of coffee. Next to the man on the bench was a white, cardboard bakery box. Ben went inside the market and walked directly to the butcher's counter at the back of the store.

John Morgan had his back to the counter and was cutting meat on a band saw. Ben waited patiently until John shut off the wicked-looking machine. "Hey, superstar," Ben said sarcastically.

John spun around with a grin. "I'm guessing you saw the paper this morning," he said.

"No, but everyone is talking about it. Way to keep a low profile."

"Garvin over at the paper called me yesterday afternoon asking if they could do a story on what happened. What could I say?"

"You could have said no."

"I did, at first, but you should have seen the look on Jenny's face when I told her Garvin had called. She's so proud of me, Ben. She made me call him back and say yes." The big man put his palms on the meat counter and leaned in closer. "We had sex last night ... and it was her idea. It's never her idea. She's treating me like I'm Clint Eastwood or something."

Ben shook his head. "Well, I'm glad you're having fun with this, but maybe it's not such a good idea to call that much attention to yourself."

John put up his hands. "Okay, okay, maybe you're right. I'm sure this is the end of it. What can I get for ya?"

"Nothing today. Just stopped in to say hey."

"Aw, that's sweet, checking up on me like that. Don't worry, I keep a squirt gun behind the counter now, just in case." John chuckled at his own joke.

"Just be careful," Ben said and headed back the way he had come.

John continued to laugh at his friend's overprotectiveness. He stepped back to the saw and flipped on the switch.

When Ben exited the grocery store the same man was still sitting on the bench drinking coffee. He watched Ben, but turned his head when their eyes met. Ben decided to cross the street and see what looked good at the bakery.

As Ben reached the other side of the street, the stranger leaned back and crossed his leg. He nodded to Ben without expression.

"Good morning," Ben said.

"Morning," the man answered.

"Beautiful day."

"Yes it is."

Ben walked up the steps and into the bakery.

"Good morning, handsome," Lita said from behind the counter. She was placing freshly baked chocolate chip cookies side by side in the display case. "How was that apple pie?"

"Good," Ben replied. "Not as good as the cherry, I'm guessing, but I wouldn't know for sure. I would have to ask the local hero about that."

Lita stuck out her bottom lip and frowned, giving Ben an exaggerated sad face. "It's more sad than terrifying when the green monster rears its ugly head."

"Who said that?"

"Me. Didn't you hear me?"

"Whatever. Who's the guy sitting out front?"

Lita craned her neck toward the front window. "What guy?"

"That guy," Ben replied as he turned to the front of the store. "The one sitting—well he *was* sitting right there."

The bench was empty. Ben walked to the door, opened it, and walked out onto the steps. He looked west, up Main Street, and then east; the stranger was gone. He stepped back inside.

"There was a guy sitting out there on the bench drinking coffee. He was tall, thin, and had blond hair. He was wearing jeans, a blue button-up shirt, and a black sport coat."

"Oh yeah, that guy," Lita recalled. "He bought a dozen oatmeal cookies and grabbed a cup of coffee."

"He pay with a credit card?"

"No, cash. Why?"

"He say where he was from?"

"No, he just said he was passing through on business. Why?"

"Just wondering."

"Okay. He seemed like a nice guy."

"I'm sure he was. I just thought I recognized him from somewhere."

"Well, if he stops in again on his way back through, I'll tell him you asked about him."

"I'd rather you didn't, Lita."

Lita shrugged. "Or not."

"Have a nice day, Lita," Ben said, and went back toward the door. "Tell Howard I said hey."

"Will do," Lita responded. "And you give your family my best."

My family, Ben thought as he walked down the steps and across the street. Not only was he beginning to think of Claire and Mica as his family, but evidently so was the rest of Dunquin Cove. He caught himself smiling as he climbed aboard the old Ford pickup and headed down the road.

Ben drove along Shore Drive in the direction of the B&B with his radio blasting sixties music. When the song set ended Larry Lincoln said, "That was *Moondance* by Van Morrison, and I'm Big Larry Lincoln. Hey, folks, as many of you may have heard, Dunquin Cove has a new local hero. John Morgan, owner of Callaway's Market over on Main Street, stopped a robbery in progress two nights ago at another local business. John will be Todd Fairman's guest this evening at five o'clock right here on 104.2. Tune in and listen to John tell how he single-handedly disarmed two masked men in a fight for survival that left one of the would-be robbers dead and the second in police custody."

Ben reached down and turned off the radio. "Oh, brother," he whispered.

Chapter Seven

Ben parked in the street and carried the pane of glass up the driveway and leaned it against the garage wall. He opened the side door and went in to see why the overhead door hadn't opened when he tried it earlier in the morning. He inspected the track on the left hand side of the door. It seemed fine, so he went to the other side; it looked good as well. *Huh,* he thought. *What could be wrong?* Grabbing the bottom of the door with both hands he gave it a yank upwards. It broke free and lifted. He lowered the door to the closed position and then raised it again with ease. His eyes went from one moving part to the other. He left the door in the up position, just in case Claire needed to go somewhere, and walked out of the garage.

Claire was standing at the sink doing the breakfast dishes when Ben walked up the steps into the kitchen. "Something wrong with the new door?" she asked.

"No. Why?" Ben answered confoundedly.

She glanced out the window and nodded her head toward the garage. "It looked like you were having trouble with it."

"Nope. Works like a charm."

Ben continued on through the kitchen and when he was halfway through the dining room, Claire asked, "Hey, did you see the write-up in the paper about John?"

"No, but I heard about it."

"From who?"

"Who didn't I hear it from?" Ben replied disgustedly.

"Sor-*ee*," said Claire. "I didn't realize it was such a touchy subject. Won't mention it again."

"Good," Ben grumbled.

"Good," Claire aped.

Ben grabbed the phone and dialed.

"Callaway's Market," a sweet old lady's voice announced. "How may I help you?"

"Alice, it's Ben Dunning. Can I—"

"Good morning, Ben," Alice interrupted. "How are you today?"

"Good, Alice. Can I talk—"

"How's Claire and Mica?"

"They're both good. Can I speak—"

"Weren't you in here earlier, Ben?"

"Yes, Alice, I was. Can I talk to John for a second?"

"I'll put you right through."

A few seconds later, John said, "John here. What can I do for you?"

"John, it's Ben."

"Hey, buddy. What's going on? Did you forget something?"

"John, don't do that radio interview tonight."

"Oh, you found out about that."

"Yes. I heard Big Larry Lincoln talking about it on the radio."

"It's no big deal, pal. They said they just wanted me to talk about how I stopped the robbery."

"John, you *didn't* stop a robbery. Remember?"

"Well, I helped."

"Yes, you did, but let's not go on the radio and brag about it."

"I'm not bragging. I'm just having a little fun with it, that's all. Nothing to worry about."

"John you gotta use your head, man. There might be someone out there who's not real happy that that boy ended up dead."

"Well, I didn't shoot him. His partner did."

"Yeah, but everyone thinks *you* did it."

"Ben, you worry too much."

"Maybe. But it's better to be safe than sorry."

"Good one. You come up with that on your own?" John asked sarcastically. "I gotta get back to work, pal. Don't worry so much. I can take care of myself."

"Just be—" Ben heard the click ending the call before he could finish his sentence. He laid the handset back in its cradle.

"Who was that?" Claire asked on her way by.

"I called John. There was something I forgot to tell him."

Claire started up the stairs. "Leave him alone. Let him have his fifteen minutes of fame."

Ben placed his hand on the door knob. "I'm going back out to the garage and fix that window."

Claire paused halfway up the stairs. "What window?"

"The window Marvin broke yesterday. I'm hoping I can get out there early enough to do it by myself." He pulled the front door open.

"Good morning, neighbor," Marvin said. He was standing on the front porch, putty knife in hand, and ready to work.

"Morning, Marvin."

"You boys have fun," Claire sang out from the top of the stairs.

"Yeah," Ben mumbled. "Fun."

The two men walked around the side of the house, across the slate stone patio, past the water fountain, and to the garage.

"Didn't know if you had a putty knife, so I brought one," said Marvin.

"I'm going to back the van out of the garage. The new piece of glass is leaning up against the wall."

After Ben backed out of the garage Marvin found a small piece of half-inch plywood and laid it on the concrete floor. Then he removed the two old rusted nails from the window stops and removed the broken sash. He gently laid the sash on the plywood and began chipping away at the old glazing compound.

"We'll have this fixed in no time," Marvin said, when he heard Ben walk up behind him. "You know who's good at glazing a window?"

"I can't imagine," Ben replied.

"Cobb."

"He is, is he?"

"Yup."

"Maybe you should give him a call," Ben said sarcastically. "We could sure use another person over here."

"Called him before I came over. He said he would be here in a minute."

"Swell."

Ben heard the back door open and looked over.

"Hey, Ben," Claire called out.

"Yeah?"

"Someone just called again and wouldn't say anything. I hung up and a few seconds later it rang again. I answered, and he asked to speak with you."

"With me?"

"Yeah."

"Did he leave a name?"

"No, but I think it was that Flannigan guy that called yesterday."

"What did you tell him?"

"I told him you were working outside and did he want me to go get you."

"And?"

"He said he would call back around five this evening. He said if he can't get a hold of you he might drive up here to see you in person."

Ben glanced down at Marvin who was in his own little world as he worked on the window. He looked up and saw Alan Cobb walking across the driveway holding his own putty knife. Then his eyes went to Mica's bike leaning up against the back of the house, and then back at Claire. "Okay," he said. "I'll make sure I'm in the house when he calls back. Thanks."

Claire stepped back inside and let the door shut behind her.

Cobb clapped his hands together. "All right," he said. "Let's get this window fixed, boys."

Chapter Eight

At quarter to five Ben turned on the radio that Claire kept on a shelf in the kitchen next to the stove. Todd Fairman, the early evening DJ was informing his listeners of the upcoming week's weather. When he finished he told everyone to stick around for the interview with "local hero, John Morgan."

Claire stepped into the kitchen. "Bring the radio into the living room so we can all hear the interview," she said.

Ben reached over, unplugged the radio, and carried it into the living room. He set it on the end table next to the big red chair that sat next to the fireplace. He bent over and reached behind the end table plugging in the radio. He turned it on; *Carefree Highway* was playing.

The phone rang and Ben said, "I'll get it in the kitchen." He walked to the kitchen and turned to make sure no one had followed him in before answering the phone. "Hello?"

"Who am I speaking with?" Flannigan asked.

"Who are you looking for?" Ben asked.

"You know who I'm looking for. I'm looking for Max Wright."

"There's no one here by that name."

"Listen … Mr. Dunning, I wouldn't have called if I didn't already know who you were. From what my people tell me, it sounds like you've got a really good thing going on up there in Maine. They tell me you've carved out a nice little spot for yourself in that community. Everyone knows you. Everyone even seems to like you. But they don't really know you, do they, Max?"

Ben said nothing.

"It's time for you to go back to work, Max," said Flannigan.

"I don't do that anymore," Ben said.

Flannigan chuckled. "So, you've retired."

"You could say that."

"I'll make it worth your while."

"Why me, Flannigan? There are others who could use the work, I'm sure."

"I want *you*, Max. I want the best."

"I'm sorry, Flannigan, but it looks like you'll have to settle for second best."

"I won't take no for an answer."

"You already have. I'm hanging up now."

"I'll give you two days to change your mind. Give me a call back when you do. Give Claire and Mica my best." The line went dead and Ben hung up.

When Ben returned to the living room the radio was still playing. Claire sat on the couch, and Mica lay across the recliner with his head resting on one arm and his legs dangling over the other. John Morgan was well into his harrowing tale.

"So there I was crouched down in the toy aisle," John said. "I could see two shadows behind the pharmacy counter at the back of the store. They were filling a sack with bottles—"

"So there were two guys behind the pharmacy counter?" Todd Fairman asked.

"Did I say two? I meant one. There was only one guy behind the counter."

"Go on."

"So I grabbed a squirt gun off the rack and when they came around to my side of the counter I shouted, 'Freeze scumbags, or I'll blow your damn heads off!' Can I say 'damn heads' on the radio, Todd?"

"You just did," Fairman chuckled.

Ben rolled his eyes. "Freeze, scumbags," he repeated.

"Shh!" said Claire.

Mica's eyes and ears were glued to the radio. Ben imagined everyone else in town had the same looks on their faces.

"Then what happened?" Fairman asked.

"They froze. Then I told them to drop the sack, and they did."

"Amazing," Fairman commented.

"Then Snake—that's what they called the big guy with the gun—he comes around the corner and tells me to drop my gun. Well, I could tell by the look on his face that I had better do as I was told. So I dropped the squirt gun. Then Snake tells—"

"That's an amazing story, John," Fairman interrupted. "We have to go to a commercial, folks, but when we return, local hero John Morgan will tell us how he felt as he stood there looking down the barrel of a loaded gun." Fairman said "loaded gun" in the most menacing tone he could muster.

A commercial for the Lobster Shack began playing. Claire looked up at Ben, who was standing in the doorway to the living room. "Wow!" she said. "I can't imagine what I would have done in his shoes."

"Yeah, me neither," said Ben.

"I wonder what he's gonna say next?" said Mica.

"I can't imagine," Ben replied.

"We're back, folks," Fairman announced. "And we have John Morgan in the studio telling us about his life or death ordeal at the drugstore last Wednesday night. So there you were, John, staring down the barrel of Snake's gun. What happened next?"

"Well, Todd, I'm not ashamed to say that I was scared."

"You had every right to be, my friend. Every right to be."

"So Snake tells the other guy to run and grab a roll of duct tape from one of the aisles. He informed me that I had seen their faces and that they were going to take me with them. I knew what that meant, Todd. It meant I was never going to see my wife and kids again. All I could think about was Jenny, and the kids. I didn't want those kids growing up without a father. I knew what I had to do."

"Wow," Ben said. "He tells a great story."

"Shh!" said Claire.

"What happened next?" Fairman asked.

"When the other guy returned with the duct tape he started to wrap it around my wrist. I knew this was my only chance. I shoved my hand into the roll of duct tape and quickly wrapped it around *his* wrists."

"Wow!" Fairman said. "You're like Jason Bourne."

"I was *just* like Jason Bourne, Todd."

"Then what?"

Mica was on the edge of his seat. Claire was gnawing away at her fingernails.

John continued, "I slung the kid around and into Snake. As Snake fell his gun discharged hitting his partner in the head. Snake's head hit the edge of the counter, knocking him out cold. There was blood everywhere. Then we called the police."

"We?" Fairman asked

"I mean me."

"That's an incredible story, John. If only there were more people like you, this would be a much safer world. You're a true hero."

"I'm no hero, Todd. I'm just a man who did what he had to do."

"You heard it, folks, just a man doing what he had to do. Thanks for coming in, John, we really enjoyed having you on."

"It was my pleasure, Todd."

"And folks, make sure you head on over to Callaway's Market on Main Street in beautiful, historic, downtown Dunquin Cove."

The radio went right to a Dunquin Cove Auto commercial; Ben walked over and shut it off. "Well, that was some story," he said.

Claire got up from the couch. "You're so jealous. Why can't you be happy for him like everyone else in town?"

"I guess I'm just a real jerk."

"I guess you are." Claire left the room and walked down the hall toward the dining room.

Mica climbed out of the big red chair and walked over to Ben. He threw his arms around him and said, "I bet you could have stopped those robbers, too, if you were there," he said.

Ben put his hand on top of the boys head. "Thanks, pal."

Chapter Nine

Ben was dressed in a brand new pair of red flannel pajama bottoms and a white T-shirt. He was slouched down in the couch with his feet on the coffee table. The television was tuned to the Boston Red Sox game.

Claire walked down the stairs and paused in the doorway to the living room. "How come you're not wearing the top I got you?" she asked.

Ben didn't take his eyes off the TV. "Well, for one thing, men do not wear tops, they wear shirts."

Claire smirked. "Okay, *man*, how come you're not wearing the matching shirt that came in the same package as the bottoms that said 'matching pajama top and bottoms' on it?"

Ben tugged at his own pant leg. "They're pants, not bottoms."

"Has this whole thing with John made you feel like less of a man?"

"No."

"But you're not confident enough in your manhood to wear matching pajamas?"

Ben turned his head and glared at Claire. "I was wearing the shirt and Mica made fun of me. He said I looked like I was going to a sleep-over."

"You're telling me that a ten-year-old boy picked on you."

"Yes. That kid's a bully. You should probably have a talk with him."

Claire turned and started back down the hall. "Oh, I will," she assured Ben. "I will." When she got to the kitchen, she called out, "Do you want a glass of milk and a couple of these cookies?"

"Is that another dig about the pajamas?"

"No."

"Then yes, I'll have some cookies and milk."

Claire brought a small plate with three cookies and a glass of milk and set them on the coffee table. Ben leaned to the side to see around her, not wanting to miss any of the seventh inning action.

"Am I in your way?" Clair asked.

"No," Ben replied.

Claire moved a little to her left, and Ben slid back to his right.

"I'm not in your way?" she asked again.

"You are now."

Claire giggled and put her knees on top of the coffee table. She slid the plate of cookies to the edge of the table. Ben wouldn't take his eyes off the television. Claire leaned forward to give Ben an unobstructed view down the front of her shirt.

Ben's eyes went to her cleavage, back to the TV, and then back to her breasts.

"Having a hard time concentrating on the game?" she asked.

Ben feigned anger. "You're an evil woman, Claire Dunning," he said, "with really nice boobs."

"If you come upstairs right now, I'll show you how evil I am."

Ben grabbed the remote control that was sitting on the cushion next to him. "Boring game anyway," he announced, hitting the power button.

Claire backed slowly off the coffee table keeping her eyes locked on Ben's, she stood and backed up toward the stairway, giving him the come-hither finger.

Ben smiled slyly as he followed.

The phone rang.

Son of a bitch, Ben thought. Who could that be at this hour? He reached for the phone that laid next to him on the small table.

"Seriously?" Claire asked.

"Colsome House Bed and Breakfast," Ben answered. "How can I help you?"

"Ben, it's John."

"Hey. What's up, buddy?"

"I just got a phone call."

Claire waited patiently on the stairs.

"Yeah, so did I. It was you. What's going on?"

"The guy on the phone said I cost him a lot of money."

"I told you the prices down at the store were a little too high."

"Be serious, Ben," John urged. "He said I cost him a lot of money and he expects payment in full."

Ben sighed. "Oh, boy." He glanced up the stairs at Claire. "I'll be there in a minute."

Claire cocked her head.

"I'll be there in an hour."

She cocked her head the other way.

"I'll be there in twenty minutes."

"But—"

Ben tossed the phone back onto its cradle and chased his woman up the stairs.

Chapter Ten

Ben took a left off of Main Street onto Maple Street and pulled to the curb in front of John and Jenny Morgan's house. It was a little after ten, and the only lights on at the Morgan place were the two living room lamps and the front porch light.

Ben climbed out of his truck and walked to the front door. He knocked three times and turned the knob. "John?" he called out quietly.

"In here," John answered.

John sat in his recliner watching the television, which was arranged in front of the picture window that looked out over Maple Street. His bolt-action .30-06 Springfield leaned against the wall next to him. An opened box of shells sat on the end table.

"Paranoid much?" Ben asked.

"Can't be too careful," John replied. "It was my dad's."

"Where's Jenny and the kids?"

"Upstairs in bed."

"Jenny know about the phone call?"

"No. I told her it was a wrong number."

"A lot of that going around." Ben walked across the room and took a seat on the sofa, adjacent to John. He glanced over at the television. "You watch the game tonight?" he asked.

John nodded. "Just ended. Went into extra innings. Pedroia hit a walk-off homer. Sox won eleven to eight."

"Dammit!"

"You missed it?"

"Claire wanted to have sex."

"You poor bastard."

"So what exactly did this guy say?" Ben asked.

"I told you what he said," John replied. "He said I cost him a lot of money, and he expects to be paid back in full."

"Did he say how much?"

"Nope. I don't think he just wants money. I think he wants revenge."

"I think you're right."

"What am I going to do?"

Ben sat back in his seat and stared at the ceiling for answers. "Let's see," he pondered, tapping his chin with his index finger. "What should a local hero, who can single-handedly disarm two would be thieves, leaving one dead, do when threatened?"

"You're a prick," said John.

Ben laughed. "This is exactly why I told you not to do the interview."

"This isn't funny," John scolded. "And I'm sorry I did the newspaper interview. It was a mistake."

"Yeah, so was the radio interview. What was your next step, rent billboards with your picture and address on them?"

John's head turned back to the TV. "The caller also knows about the Reilly kid being involved in the robbery."

"What did he say about that?"

"He asked if Donny Reilly was a friend of mine, and if that's why I let him go. He thinks Donny told me about the robbery and that we planned to take the stolen pills and sell them ourselves."

"What did you tell him?"

"I told him I had no idea what he was talking about."

"Did he believe you?"

"I don't think so. He kind of chuckled when I said it, and said, 'Lying is no way to score points.'"

Ben guffawed. "Honesty is always the best policy," he said.

"Says the guy who took off and had me take all the credit."

"So this is my fault?"

"Of course it's your fault!" John hollered. He caught himself and then whispered, "Of course it's your fault. Do you know how many gun-involved incidents I've been in since you moved to town? Three, that's how many. I've lived here more than half my life. Know how many I was involved in before you came here? Zero!"

"So you're saying your life has gotten a lot more exciting since I moved here?"

John glared at his amnesiac friend. "You've changed since you first gotten here. You would have taken something like this a lot more serious a year ago."

Ben locked his fingers behind his head, leaned back on the couch, and crossed his legs. "Yeah, I think you're right. I feel myself developing a more laid-back attitude toward things. I figure it's due to small town living. I may even start wearing flip-flops and listening to Jimmy Buffett."

"Yeah, whatever. What are we going to do?"

Ben yawned. "I'm going to go home. I'm tired. You go on up to bed. Nothing's going to happen tonight. Whoever this is might just be pissed and trying to scare you. We'll head out to Reilly's Feed Store tomorrow and have a talk with Donny and his old man. Maybe Donny knows who this guy is."

"So you really don't think this guy would show up here tonight?"

"I'm 90 percent sure," Ben said, pointing at the Springfield. "Besides, you got ol' blue there to protect you." Ben got up and walked toward the door. "If you need me, just call. And if I don't get here in time, use some of that judo or karate or whatever you used at the drugstore the other night."

John got up and walked Ben to the door. "After this is over, I don't think we can be friends anymore."

Ben laughed. "After this is over, I'll probably be your *best* friend … after ol' blue, I mean."

Chapter Eleven

Reilly's Feed Store located at the corner of Coffin Lane and Route 4 in the eastern most tip of Berwick, Maine. Ben and John drove over from Dunquin Cove on Thursday morning; it was a thirty-minute drive.

Ben took a right onto Coffin Lane and steered the old pickup into the parking lot. Reilly's Feed consisted of a few large green pole barns and three steel grain silos. On one of the silos the name Reilly was painted in big red letters, and underneath, the year 1968.

Ben parked his truck to the right of the office door and the two men went inside.

"Good morning," said the tall thin man behind the counter. The guy was dressed in gray coveralls and wore a Reilly Feed cap. Above the breast pocket of his coverall was the name Hal. Ben guessed Hal's age at somewhere around fifty.

"What can I do for you gentlemen today?" Hal asked.

"We're looking for Donny Reilly," Ben replied. "Is he around?"

"Who wants to know?" asked Hal.

Ben looked around the room, and then back at the man. "Well, that would be us," he said. "Are you Donny's father?"

The man pushed an intercom button on a speaker near the desk phone, leaned over a little, and spoke. "Arnold, Mike ... can you boys come to the office for a second."

Ben's eyes went to a push broom leaning against the desk, and then to an antique tractor paperweight on the desk. A heavy-duty stapler also caught his eye. "Calling for backup?" he asked.

John put up his hands. "Whoa, whoa," he said. "Let's not get crazy here, sir. We just need to ask Donny a couple questions."

Hal pointed a long, bony finger at John. "I told the last guy if any of you druggies step foot on my property again the shit was gonna hit the fan."

The door opened behind Ben and two large men stepped inside the room. They wore coveralls that matched Hal's. Their name tags read Mike and Arnold.

"Everything okay, Mr. Reilly?" Mike asked.

Ben turned and took two steps away from the two men.

"I was just asking these two men to leave," Hal answered.

"Mr. Reilly," John said. "We're not … druggies, or whatever you think we are. We're here to help Donny. It's important that we find him."

Hal looked to his employees. "Mike, Arnold, will you please show these gentlemen to their vehicle, please?"

Mike took a step toward Ben.

"Don't do it, Mike," Ben said.

Mike grinned. He was ready to kick some ass.

"Seriously, Mike," said Ben.

Mike adopted a prize fighter's stance.

"Last warning, Mike."

"Really," John said. "We're here to help Donny."

"If Donny needs help, I'll help him," his father replied. "Now get back to your vehicle on your own, or with Mike and Arnold's assistance. Your choice."

Mike swung a right at Ben, and Ben blocked it with his left, and then brought the palm of his right hand up into Mike's chin, snapping the big guys head back. Mike stumbled back a few steps, blinked a couple times, and shook his head. The back of his neck was quickly stiffening.

"You're going to feel that tomorrow, Mike," Ben informed him.

Mike worked his jaw back and forth.

Arnold moved toward Ben. John stuck out his foot, tripping him.

As Arnold tumbled forward, Ben grabbed the stapler off the desk and smacked Arnold on top of the head five times, planting five quarter-inch staples in the man's scalp.

"Ow!" Arnold screamed. He hit the floor on his knees.

Ben grabbed the push broom and smacked the handle against the side of Arnolds head, knocking him unconscious. He snapped the broom handle in half over his knee and pointed the jagged edge at Mike. "Mike, I don't want to put this in your eye, but I will."

Mike raised his hands over his head in surrender.

Ben turned the broomstick on Hal "Where's your boy?"

"It's okay, Dad," came a voice from a doorway behind the desk. "These are the guys that let me go the other night."

Mike slowly put down his arms and Hal relaxed his shoulders. Ben could feel the tension leave the room.

"If it wasn't for them," Donny explained. "I would be sitting in jail right now."

Ben stuck out his hand. "Ben Dunning," he said.

Hal shook Ben's hand.

Ben nodded his head toward John. "This is John Morgan."

Hal nodded. "So, why does my son need you two's help?"

"The man Donny and his friends were stealing pills for," John explained, "contacted me last night. He says I owe him for the pills because I stopped the robbery."

Hal looked at Ben. "What about you, you were there too."

"He doesn't know I was there," Ben replied. "As far as he knows, John stopped the robbery, and let Donny go. He thinks John and Donny were in on it together. He thinks they planned to take the pills and sell them themselves."

"We weren't in on nothin' together," Donny blurted out.

Hal shook his head. "You've really done it this time, boy."

"I'm sorry, Dad," Don said.

Hal looked from John to Ben. "He was never like this before his mother died."

"Donny, you have to tell us who you guys were working for," said Ben.

"I have no idea," Donny replied. "Jack didn't know either. Snake was the only one who knew that."

"Snake never called the guy by name?" John asked.

Donny shook his head. "No. Snake always just called the guy his friend. He would say, 'My friend wants us to do this,' or, 'My friend wants us to do that.' He never said a name."

"How long have you known Snake?" Ben asked.

"About a year. Jack introduced me to him."

"How did you know Jack?"

Donny got a shameful look on his face and glanced over at his dad. "I met him a little over a year ago when I was in juvie."

"Never like this before his mother died," repeated Hal.

"Why were you in juvie?" Ben asked.

"Went joyriding in a stolen car."

Arnold moaned and slowly climbed to his knees. He looked up at Ben; trails of blood ran down his face from the staples in his head. Ben reached down and helped the guy to his feet.

"Up you go, big fella," Ben said. "Why don't you run in the bathroom and have Mike pull those out of your head." He saw a wand-style staple remover in a plastic caddy on Hal's desk. "Here," Ben said, putting it in Arnold's paw, "use this."

"Thanks," Arnold said.

"Can we go, Mr. Reilly?" Mike asked.

"Yeah," Hal responded. "Put some Bactine on those holes. You don't want that to get infected."

"They still make Bactine?" Ben asked.

"Yeah, I sell it at the store," said John.

"Huh," Ben said. He returned his attention to Donny. "How many places have you robbed with Snake?"

"Cecil's place was the third."

Hal shook his head. "Cecil was always good to you, boy. He gave you a job, and look how you repaid him."

"I'm sorry."

"You're sorry, all right."

"You live close by?" Ben asked.

Hal pointed up the street. "Right up here at the end of Coffin Lane," he replied.

"You have a gun?"

"I got a .30-30, and an old 20-gauge."

"You might want to keep them handy in case Snake's friend comes looking for Donny."

"Maybe we should call the police," Hal suggested.

"And then your boy goes to jail for the robbery at the pharmacy," Ben responded.

Hal slammed his hand down on the counter. "Dammit, boy! I'm glad your mother ain't here to see this."

"Sor—"

"Don't say it again, boy."

"Listen, Donny," said Ben, "everything is going to be okay. If he contacts you, you call me." Ben grabbed a pencil that was lying on the desk next to the cash register, and then pointed at a note pad. Hal slid the note pad in front of Ben. Ben jotted down two phone numbers. "This top number is mine, and the other is John's at the store." Ben slid the pad back to Hal.

"What if he just shows up here?" Hal asked.

"Then do what you gotta do," Ben replied.

Chapter Twelve

After returning to Dunquin Cove, Ben dropped John off at the market and then drove home. When he pulled up in front of the B&B he noticed the black Lincoln Town Car parked across the street. Ben drove past the Colsome House and took a right onto Harp Street. He pulled to the curb and shut off the engine; he wished he were carrying his 9mm.

Ben climbed out of the truck and walked through the neighbor's backyard into the backyard of the B&B. He stood next to the garage watching the back of the house. The garage door was open. Ben quickly walked to the back of the garage and grabbed a large Phillips head screwdriver off the workbench and shoved it into his back pocket. He hurried to the back door and went inside.

Standing in the kitchen, Ben could hear Claire's voice coming from the living room. She sounded okay. Her voice wasn't stressed or shaky. Ben heard another voice, masculine. The man laughed, and then Claire let out a chuckle of her own. Ben relaxed a little.

Ben didn't even try to be quiet as he made his way through the kitchen and down the hall; he knew the old floorboards would give him away.

"This must be him now," Claire announced, as Ben was almost to the living room.

Ben stepped into the doorway. Claire sat on the sofa and a dark-haired man in a navy-blue suit sat in the puffy red chair. The man's hair was parted on the side and every hair was in place. His fingers had been recently manicured. His face was tan, and his Italian shoes cost more than Ben's old truck. The man looked up and smiled when he saw Ben enter the room. His teeth were white and perfect. Laugh lines appeared around his eyes. Claire looked up and smiled as well, but her smile was real. The unknown man had a nice smile, and most people would be fooled, but Ben knew better. There was evil in this man's grin, and even more in his eyes. Ben knew this was Neil Flannigan.

"Ben," Claire said, "this is Mr. Flannigan."

"Neil," Flannigan said.

Ben nodded.

"He drove up from Boston," said Claire. "He still hasn't heard from his friend—" Claire looked to Flannigan for a name.

"Max Wright," said Flannigan. He stared into Ben's eyes searching for some kind of reaction, but Ben was better than that.

"You don't say," Ben responded. "Maybe he's avoiding you." Ben did his best to duplicate the smile Flannigan had given him.

"I would hope not," Flannigan responded.

"How well did you know this … Max Wright, you say?" Ben asked.

"He worked for me on a couple occasions."

"So you were business acquaintances," Claire said.

"You could say that," Flannigan replied.

"Have you ever met him in person?" Ben asked.

"No," Flannigan said. "Not actually in person. We communicated through emails and by telephone."

Ben's eyes were locked on Flannigan's. He wondered if Flannigan was carrying a weapon. *Of course he is*, Ben thought. Ben also knew he could remove the Phillips screwdriver from his back pocket and throw it into Flannigan's heart before the man could even reach inside his jacket. But who knew he was here and who might come next?

"Then how will you know him when you see him?" Ben asked.

"I'll know." Flannigan put his hands on his knees. "Well, I guess I better hit the road."

Without looking away from Flannigan, Ben took a couple steps back, reached over, and opened the front door. "I'll walk you to your car."

"That's very kind of you, Mr. Dunning." Flannigan got up and turned to Claire. "It was very nice to meet you Claire. Ben is one lucky man."

Ben and Neil Flannigan walked down the steps and across the street to Flannigan's Lincoln. Ben looked over his shoulder as he walked. Claire was watching out the front window.

When Flannigan got to the car door he turned around.

Ben spoke through his teeth. "You ever show up at my home again and I'll put a bullet through your head."

"Don't threaten me, Max," Flannigan warned.

"What do you want with me?" Ben asked.

"I've already told you. I want to hire you for a job."

"I told you, I don't do that anymore."

"You don't even know what it is." Flannigan stared into Ben's eyes. "There's something different about you, Max."

"I thought you said we had never met."

"It's the way you speak to me, like you've never spoken to me before. Like you're pretending to know who I am, or playing the part of someone who used to know me."

"I don't know what you're talking about," said Ben.

"You're not even sure if we've ever met, are you, Max?"

Ben didn't answer.

"What happened to you?" Flannigan asked.

Ben turned around and started to walk away. Flannigan grabbed his shoulder. Ben came up with an elbow knocking Flannigan's arm away. Both men grabbed each other by the front of their shirts. Ben pushed Flannigan back against his car.

Flannigan released Ben and put up his hands. "You're making a big mistake, Max," he said.

"It's you who's making the mistake, Flannigan." Ben released his grip, turned, and started across the street.

"Someone murdered my son," said Flannigan.

Ben paused and turned around.

"Max, someone killed my son, Carl," Flannigan repeated, "his girlfriend, her mother, and three of his friends."

"What are you talking about?" Ben asked.

"My stepson, Carl, he was visiting his girlfriend at her mother's home in Dorchester. A man came in and killed them all."

"This man, do you know who he is?"

"If I knew who he was, he would already be dead. That's what I want you to find out, Max. I want you to find this man, bring him to me, and I want to kill him … slowly, and painfully."

"Why would someone want to kill your son?"

"Let's face it, Max, I have more enemies than friends."

"Did anybody see this man enter or leave the house?"

"A neighbor gave the cops a brief description. About five-ten, five-eleven, with brown hair and medium build."

"That doesn't really narrow it down," Ben pointed out. "Hell, it could be anyone."

"I'll make it worth your while, Max," Flannigan said.

"I'm sorry for your loss, Flannigan, but like I said, I'm no longer in that line of work."

Flannigan looked over Ben's shoulder at the bed and breakfast. "So this is you now. You're an innkeeper."

"For now," Ben replied. He turned and walked back to the house.

Flannigan stood in the street and watched until the door closed behind Ben, then he climbed into the Lincoln and drove down the street.

Ben leaned back against the inside of the front door, remembering the day he burst into the home on Bloomfield Street in Dorchester to save Maggie and her mother. He remembered every bullet he put into Carl and his three cronies. He also remembered Maggie and her mother being alive when he left the house. He knew Flannigan and his men had probably killed them in an attempt to get information.

"Is everything okay?" Claire asked.

"Yes," Ben replied.

"What were you guys talking about?"

"Small town life."

Chapter Thirteen

Around six-thirty Thursday evening Ben took a right onto Main Street, drove to the end, and made a U-turn. He parked his truck in front of Callaway's Market. As Ben exited his truck he looked across the street at the man sitting on the bench in front of Lita's Bakery; it was the same man who had been sitting there Tuesday morning. The guy was wearing the same suit, or one that looked just like it.

Ben's eyes went to the plate glass window in the front of bakery. Lita stood in the window pointing down at the guy, her finger making a vigorous jabbing motion. It was all Ben could do not to laugh. He nodded his head and started across the street toward the stranger.

"Good morning," Ben said, when he reached the curb.

"Good morning," the man replied. He sat sipping his coffee. A white bakery box sat on the bench next to him just like the last time.

Ben pointed at the box. "More half-moons?"

The man nodded. "Can't get enough of 'em."

"They're like a drug."

The man grinned. "Yes, they are."

"I suppose your boss has you sitting here to watch my friend John Morgan."

"You mean local hero, John Morgan."

"Yes," said Ben. He looked around to make sure no one was within earshot. "You go back to wherever it is you came from, and tell your boss that he'll have his pills Saturday morning."

"And how exactly is that going to happen?"

"Don't worry about it," Ben replied. "Just tell him to contact John with a meeting place, and we'll deliver the pills to him in person."

"You'll deliver the pills to me," said the man.

"It's your boss, or no one. His choice."

The man stood. He was three inches taller than Ben. "I'll let him know."

"And one more thing. If I ever see you in this town again, I'll kill you."

The man snickered and started to poke Ben in the chest. "Don't make threats you can't—"

Ben grabbed the man's finger and bent it backwards. There was a loud snap. Ben brought his thumb up into the man's jugular at the same time he hit him in the balls with his knee. The big man cried out and dropped to his knees.

Ben kept twisting the finger. He leaned over and pressed his thumb into the man's throat even harder. Ben's nose was inches from the tough guy's nose. "That wasn't a threat. That was a promise." Ben gave the man another knee, this time to the chest. He fell backwards to the sidewalk. "You have a nice day … and enjoy those half-moons."

Ben jogged up the stairs and into the bakery. "Any apple pie today, Lita?" he asked.

Lita remained silent as she watched Ben cross the room to the glass display counter. He examined its contents.

Lita's head turned slowly back to the window. She watched as the guy out front climbed to his feet and staggered to his car.

"Lita," Ben called out.

Lita's head snapped around. "What?"

"Any apple pie?"

"One just came out of the oven," she replied. Her eyes went to the window again, and then back to Ben. "I'm guessing I just lost a customer."

"Yeah," said Ben. "He probably won't be back."

"He seemed like a nice guy."

"He wasn't."

"I'll take your word for it."

"Thank you. Should I come back for that pie?"

"Are you going to be in town for a while?"

"I have to run across the street to Callaway's and talk to John for a minute."

"Okay," Lita offered. "I'll let it cool for a while and then box it up for you. You can pick it up after."

"Thanks, Lita." Ben started for the door.

"You're welcome, Ben."

Ben stopped at the door, but didn't turn around. "And, Lita …"

"Yes, Ben?"

"Can we just keep that little thing that happened out front between you and I?"

"Ayuh."

Ben let the door shut behind him and made his way across the street to the market.

John Morgan was right where he always was, behind the meat counter. He was wearing his usual bloodstained apron that called to mind *The Texas Chainsaw Massacre*. "Hey, buddy," he said, when he saw Ben walk out of the produce aisle. "How're they hangin'?"

Ben never knew how to answer that question. He knew it had to do with testicles, but why would anyone ask that?

"What's up?" Ben responded. "Any word from the pissed of drug dealer?"

"Not today."

Ben threw a thumb over his shoulder toward Lita's. "There's been a guy staked out over on Lita's bench for the last few days. He's been watching you."

"Me?" John asked concernedly.

"Yeah. I just spoke with him before I came over."

"What did you say?"

"I told him to tell his boss that we would have his pills for him the day after tomorrow."

"You told him that?"

"I also told him that we would deliver them in person."

"Deliver them where?"

"You'll be getting a call to let you know where."

"When will that be?"

"I don't know, so make sure you stay by your phone."

John looked up at the clock. "I'll be closing up at seven. I'll head right home."

"Cecil close up the pharmacy at seven also?" Ben asked.

"I'm pretty sure."

"How about you have someone else close up tonight and you and I will go talk to Cecil before he closes."

"About what?"

"About giving us a shit load of pills."

"Oh, crap."

Chapter Fourteen

"Are you out of your mind!" Cecil hollered.

"Keep it down, Cecil," John said. "Jeez."

Ben leaned his back against the pharmacy counter with his arms crossed over his chest.

"You want me to hand every pill in the pharmacy over to you?" said Cecil.

"Not every pill," John said. "Just the good ones."

"The good ones?" Cecil asked.

Ben began listing the pills. "Xanax, Valium, Ativan, Klono—"

"I know what the good ones are," Cecil said. "I've been a pharmacist for over forty years."

"We're just borrowing the pills," John said.

"That's the plan," Ben agreed.

"And what if something goes wrong?" Cecil asked. "I could go to prison."

"We'll make it look like you were robbed," Ben said. "Open late on Saturday, after noon. We should be back by then. If we're not, call the police and tell them you were robbed."

"I don't know," Cecil said, shaking his head and staring into the floor.

"Remember last year when Ben ran those assholes from Patrelli and Pert out of town?" John reminded Cecil. "We all would have been in some deep shit if he hadn't."

"Yes," Cecil replied. "Of course I remember."

"Now you owe Ben a favor."

"You don't owe me anything Cecil," Ben said. "I'm just asking."

"Okay, okay. When will you pick up the pills?

"You leave the back door unlocked when you close up tomorrow night," Ben instructed. "John and I will come in and take what we need."

"I'm trusting you on this, Ben," Cecil said.

"Everything will be fine," John assured him.

"Famous last words," Cecil grumbled. He glanced down at his wrist watch. "I gotta lock up and get out of here."

As the three men walked toward the front of the store, Ben put his hand on Cecil's back. "Don't worry about a thing, Cecil," he said.

"I worry about everything, Ben," Cecil replied. "That's just the kind of guy I am."

When they got outside, Cecil went directly to his '74 El Camino and drove away.

"I love that car," John commented.

"Who wouldn't?" said Ben.

"Someone told me he got that car brand new from his parents when he graduated from college."

"You don't say."

"All I got was an attaboy."

"Better than a kick in the ass."

"What did your parents get you for graduation?"

"I have no idea, John."

"Oh, yeah. Sorry."

"Don't worry about it."

"I don't mean to pry, but do you even know who your parents are?"

"Nope. Too many aliases and name changes. I wouldn't know where to start looking. I don't even know if they're alive."

John reached into his shirt pocket and pulled out a White Owl cigar. He wet the tip and rolled it around in his mouth. He grabbed his lighter out of his front pocket and puffed. "God, these are horrible," he said, and proceeded to puff out a volley of smoke rings with smug satisfaction.

"Then why do you smoke them?" Ben asked, a little irritated.

"Too cheap to buy the good ones."

"Sounds about right."

"What now?"

"I think I'll head home."

"Want to grab a drink at The Cove first?"

"Good idea," Ben said.

The two men crossed the street. As they got to the sidewalk, Howard was walking backwards through the bakery door. Howard inserted the key into the lock and pulled the door shut.

"What's up, Howard?" John asked.

Howard spun around startled. "Don't sneak up on a guy like that. Jeepers."

"Sorry. I thought you heard us."

"We're going to grab a drink at The Cove," Ben said. "Care to join us?"

"Good idea," Howard said.

"That's what we thought," said John.

The three men walked the half a block to The Cove and disappeared through the front door.

Chapter Fifteen

"You want me to do what?" asked Chief of Police Chet Rose. "Are you out of your mind?"

"That's a little harsh," John replied.

"I wasn't talking to *you*," Chet said. "I know you're out of *your* mind. I was asking Ben."

The three men were in Chet's office. Chet sat at his desk, and Ben and John sat in two wooden chairs across from him. Officer Stella Raines sat at her desk and tried her best to hear the conversation through the glass panel of the old wooden door.

"It'll only take an hour, tops," Ben explained. "He shows up, we hand him the drugs, and you arrest him."

"Oh, it's that simple," Chet responded sarcastically. "And where are you going to get the drugs to give him? If you're not handing him actual drugs, there's no crime, and I can't arrest him."

"One step ahead of you," said John.

"So you think," Chet responded.

"We'll get the pills, Chet," Ben said, "but the less you know about that, the better."

"The less I know about it?" Chet questioned. "I'm the damn police chief. I shouldn't know less about anything."

"You have to trust us," Ben said.

"Trust you," Chet repeated.

"Famous last words."

"Ha-ha," John chuckled. "That's what Cecil said."

Ben cringed.

"Cecil?" Chet asked. "What does Cecil have to do with this?"

Ben rubbed his temples.

"You're getting the pills from Cecil," Chet surmised.

John looked apologetically at Ben. "Sorry."

"Listen, Chet," Ben explained. "If worse comes to worst, and something goes wrong, you arrest John and me as well."

"Wait. What?" said John.

"Oh, don't worry about that," Chet assured. "If something goes wrong, you two will be wearing cuffs quicker than"—Chet searched for a metaphor—"well, pretty damn quick."

"Quicker than flies on shit," John offered.

"Yeah, that," said Chet. "So, where and when?"

"We won't know until he calls John with instructions," Ben replied. "I had hoped we would hear from him last night, but my guess is somewhere between here and York Harbor. You'll just have to have everyone on standby."

"Everyone," Chet responded. "You mean all four of us. I can take Devlin and Marx, but I'll have to leave Stella here in town just in case."

Stella threw her arms in the air. "Oh yeah!" she hollered. "I'll just stay here and answer the damn phones. I'm a real cop, ya know. I ain't no secretary."

The three men stared out through the glass as Stella threw her tantrum.

"I know you're a real cop!" Chet yelled back. "You remind me every goddamn day."

"I didn't know she was a real cop," John said.

"She carries a gun, John," said Chet. "How many secretaries carry a gun?"

"Just the cool ones, I guess." John felt his cell phone vibrate, and reached into his pocket to get it. "Hello?" he answered.

"John Morgan?" came a voice from the earpiece.

John sat up straight in the chair. "Yes, it's me," he replied. His voice cracked a little.

"I assume everything is still on for tomorrow morning?"

"Yes."

"Good. Drive south on Shore Drive. Less than a mile out of town you'll come to an old dirt road, it'll be on your right, about three hundred yards past the Seawatch Path turn-off. At the end of the road, there is a clearing. Be there at nine o'clock. Pull anything stupid, and someone will die."

The phone call ended and John stuck the cell back in his pocket. "Nine o'clock tomorrow morning," he said. "And if we try anything stupid, someone is going to die."

"I better call the funeral home," said Chet.

"Are you saying I'm going to do something stupid?" John asked.

Chet cocked his head and stared at the big guy. There was no need to answer that.

Chapter Sixteen

At eight thirty on Saturday morning Ben Dunning drove his old Ford pick-up along Shore Drive. John Morgan sat in the passenger seat. Between them was a small black duffel bag filled with prescription medication. Between Ben and the bag, a walkie-talkie lay on the seat. John's .30-06 lay on the floor, pushed up against the seat.

Cecil had left the back door to the drugstore unlocked, just like he said he would. Ben and John entered the store around midnight, took what they needed, and left, locking the door behind them. The entire faux robbery took less than fifteen minutes.

John breathed in deep and exhaled loudly.

Ben glanced over at his friend. John's face was little more pale than usual. "Nervous?" Ben asked.

"A little," John replied. "I didn't sleep at all last night."

Ben leaned forward and turned on the radio. Glenn Frey was right in the middle of "Smuggler's Blues." Ben let out a snort.

John reached over and shut the radio off. "I hope Chet and the others are in place."

"Everything is going to be fine," Ben said. He picked up the walkie-talkie and keyed the mic. "We're two minutes out."

"Roger that," came Chet's voice from the speaker. "We're in position."

"What did I tell you?" said Ben. "They're in position."

"Now I feel better," said John.

"That didn't sound very convincing." Ben pulled to the side of the road and came to a stop at the end of the dirt road. The dirt road was pretty much a glorified footpath, and had no road sign at the intersection. It went straight back into the woods about a hundred yards and then veered off to the right. The clearing the unknown man spoke of could not be seen from Shore Road.

"Must be it," John stated.

"Uh huh," Ben replied.

Ben backed the truck up a few feet, turned right, and headed slowly and cautiously down the road.

They hadn't gone more than twenty feet when John's cell phone rang. He reached into his pocket for it and looked at the caller ID.

"Who is it?" Ben asked.

"I don't know," John replied.

"Better answer it."

"Hello?" John asked.

"They got my boy," Hal said. "They got Donny."

"Hal?" John asked. "Who has Donny? What are you talking about?"

"The drug dealer that Donny and his buddies were working for," Hal explained. "They took him."

"When did this happen?"

"Some time in the middle of the night. I went in to wake him up for work and he was gone. There was a note on his nightstand that said *I took your boy as insurance. You'll get him back when I get my drugs back*. The note also said not to call the police."

"Don't worry, Hal," John said. "We'll get Donny back."

John hung up the cell and looked at Ben for answers. "They got Donny."

"Yeah, I heard," said Ben. He grabbed the walkie-talkie. "Chet, we got a problem."

"What do you mean, *problem*?" Chet asked.

"They kidnapped Donny Reilly last night," Ben explained. "They have him with them."

"Who the hell is Donny Reilly?"

"It's a long story, but they took him to make sure we didn't try anything stupid."

"You mean like what we're trying?"

"Exactly. It's a swap now. Donny for the pills."

"Great."

"Let's just stick to the plan," Ben said. He dropped the walkie on the seat next to him.

When Ben and John reached the clearing at the end of the dirt road, Ben shut off the engine. The natural clearing had a diameter of roughly fifty yards, surrounded on all sides by ash, poplar, and butternut trees. A brook, about eight inches deep, ran lazily through the center of the clearing.

The two men got out of the truck and Ben scanned the tree line for Chet, Marx, and Devlin; they were well hidden. They left the doors open, and John stood partially behind his for cover.

"How long you think we'll have to wait?" John asked.

"Not long, I hope," Ben replied. He adjusted the 9mm he had stuffed in the back of his waistband.

Just then a black Hummer drove out of a small path on the other side of the brook.

"This must be our guy," said John.

The big vehicle came to a stop and two men climbed out of the back seat. One guy walked around the front of the Hummer; the other stayed by his door. Both men surveyed the surrounding area. The man who stayed near his door reached one arm back inside and yanked Donny Reilly out of the Hummer. The young boy hit the ground on his side with a heavy thud.

The thug grabbed Donny by his collar. "Get up!" he spat.

Ben and John watched as Donny slowly got to his feet. Even from that distance Ben could see the blood and bruises on Donny's face.

Donny was led to the front of the truck and forced to his knees.

The passenger side door opened and out climbed a third man, tall and muscular. His black hair was slicked back to his scalp. He wore blue jeans, sneakers, and a blue zip-up hoodie over his white T-shirt.

"Must be casual dress day at the mobster office," John whispered.

Blue Hoodie walked toward the front of the Hummer.

"Mr. Elliott!" someone shouted from the trees.

Ben's head spun to his right as everyone's eyes went toward the sound.

"Mr. Elliott!" came the voice again.

Chet, Marx, and Devlin all exited the woods, their hands in the air.

"They were hiding in the woods, Mr. Elliott," said one of the two men escorting Chet and the others from the forest. The man speaking was holding his weapon on the men. The other man carried Devlin's rifle at his side. Chet glanced over at Ben; he looked more embarrassed than scared. Ben knew it should be the other way around.

Elliott walked up next to Donny and stopped. "I brought the boy!" Elliott shouted. "Where's my pills?"

"They're in the back of the truck!" Ben shouted back.

Chet and the other two officers were placed on their knees next to Donny. The guy with Devlin's rifle stood behind the row of kneeling men. The other man stood at the end of the line, next to Chet.

"Well, let's get this thing moving then," said Elliott. "Get my stuff."

"Let them go," Ben ordered.

Elliott calmly reached inside his hoodie and pulled out a chrome .38 snub-nose revolver. He pointed it at Donny and fired one round into the boy's temple.

"Jesus Christ!" John shouted.

Donny fell dead on his side, on top of Devlin. Devlin tried to get up.

Elliott trained the gun on Devlin. "Don't be stupid," he said.

Devlin looked to Chet for help. Chet stared straight ahead.

"For the last time, gentlemen," Elliott said, "get my stuff." A note of exasperation had crept into his tone.

John gulped. "It looks like it's now or never." He and Ben walked down opposite sides of the truck to the rear.

"Hey," Ben whispered across the truck bed. "They're not letting any of us out of here alive." He picked up the duffel bag. "When I start shooting, you grab that rifle and do the same … as quick as you can aim and fire."

John took a deep breath and held it for a second. He exhaled and said, "Okey-dokey."

"Aim for the torso," Ben said. "It's the biggest target."

Ben turned and started across the clearing.

John stood next to the open passenger side door.

Elliott waited impatiently. All eyes were on Ben.

When Ben came to the brook, he stepped cautiously into the water, making sure not to slip on the moss-covered rocks. His eyes went from man to man in the group before him. He was deciding which one to kill first.

Devlin, Marx, and Chet were all on their knees, about five feet in front of the Hummer. Elliott stood to their right, his revolver at his side. Donny's dead body lay between Devlin and Elliott. A goon was standing behind Elliot, and another was to his left behind Devlin. The thug holding Devlin's rifle stood behind Chet. The second man who escorted the officers from the woods was standing next to Chet. Only Elliott, the guy behind him, and the man behind Devlin had their weapons drawn.

"Hurry up!" Elliott shouted.

Ben exited the brook and kept walking straight for Elliott. He held the bag in front of him with his left hand.

"That's far enough," said Elliott.

Ben halted.

"Put the bag on the ground and unzip it," Elliott ordered.

Ben complied, but as he rose from the duffel bag, he reached behind his back and pulled his 9mm from his waistband.

Elliott's eyes widened; he brought up his own gun.

It was too late. Ben fired a round into Elliott's forehead, sending him stumbling backwards. He was dead before he hit the ground.

John reached into the cab of the truck and grabbed his rifle.

Ben fired again, hitting the man behind Elliott in the chest.

Chet jumped to his feet and tackled the guy next to him.

John pulled the trigger of the old .30-06. The bullet pierced the Hummer's windshield, killing the driver instantly. His head snapped back and then fell against the steering wheel. The maddening whine of the horn filled the air.

Devlin turned and lunged toward the guy holding his rifle.

Ben and John both fired simultaneously, their bullets striking the man behind Chet. Ben hit him in the throat. John's bullet shattered his hipbone. The goon slammed against the hood of the Hummer and fell to the ground.

Devlin wrestled rifle from the other goon's grip and slammed the butt against his head. He dropped to his knees and Devlin whisked the barrel around. "Don't move, motherfucker" he panted.

Chet rolled his man over onto his belly, delivered two sharp jabs to his kidneys, and reached for his cuffs. "You're under arrest, scumbag!" he screamed.

John walked across the field and joined the others as Marx placed handcuffs on Devlin's man.

"Nice shot through the windshield," Ben said.

"Yeah," John said. "I was aiming for the guy behind Elliott."

Chet stood next to Ben. His eyes went from one dead body to the other, finally stopping on Donny. He stared at the young boy, knowing he would soon be notifying his father. "He shows up, you hand him the pills, and I arrest him," Chet said, recalling the earlier conversation with Ben. "You were right, it was less than an hour."

Chapter Seventeen

It was well after two that afternoon before the bodies were cleared from the woods and taken to the funeral home for storage. Dunquin Cove didn't have a hospital, much less a morgue. Chet decided that Cecil's prescriptions would be returned to him immediately, instead of being entered into evidence. Many rules had been broken that morning, and Chet figured one more wouldn't hurt.

Ben pulled his truck to the curb on Shore Drive in front of the Colsome House Bed and Breakfast, shut off the engine and climbed out. He walked through the three-foot wrought iron gate and up the walkway to the front door.

The big old house was quiet when he stepped inside.

"Claire!" Ben called out. He peeked into the living room as he walked down the hall. He glanced up the stairway. "Claire!" There was still no answer. "Mica!"

On his way through the dining room, Ben looked to his right into Claire's office, and to his left out the window onto the slate patio. There was no sign of Claire or Mica.

In the kitchen Ben looked out the window, over the sink, and into the backyard. Claire's van was in the garage. He shouted Claire's name down the cellar stairs. He opened the refrigerator and grabbed two Bud Light longnecks between his fingers and headed out the back door.

Ben held the two beers in his left hand and pounded on Marvin's front door with his right. He could hear Marvin yelling, "I'm coming, I'm coming!"

Marvin flung the door open with a flatulent creak.

"What do ya need?" he asked in his signature petulant tone.

Ben held up the beers. "Brought you a beer," he said.

"It ain't my birthday," said Marvin. He stepped out onto the porch and snatched one of the bottles away from Ben. "Have a seat." Marvin motioned toward the two plastic lawn chairs that sat to his right.

Ben sat down in one of the chairs and Marvin sat in the other.

"Where were you all morning?" Marvin asked.

Ben relived the shootout in his head. "John and I took a ride. He was looking for a fishing spot someone had told him about."

Marvin sipped his beer. "Oh yeah? Whereabouts?"

"Out on Shore Drive, near Seawatch Path. There's a dirt road that leads back to a small stream."

"Rush Swamp Brook," Marvin offered. "Ain't no fish in there."

"You know of it?"

"I know every stream, brook, river, lake, and pond within two hundred miles," Marvin said. "One of the benefits of being older than dirt."

Ben laughed.

"Where's Claire and the boy today?" Marvin asked.

Ben shrugged and sipped his drink. "Claire must have gone for a walk or something. Not sure where Mica is. Probably at a friend's house."

"Least he ain't sitting in the house on the interweb playin' those damn TV games like most kids today."

Alan Cobb's front door opened and the old Vietnam vet walked out onto his front porch. Ben and Marvin raised their beers. Cobb waved, and held up the old wait-a-minute finger. He stepped back inside the house and returned a few minutes later with a drink of his own. Cobb walked across the street with his rum and Coke in hand.

"You guys hear what happened out on Shore Drive this morning?" Cobb asked.

"No, ya gossipy old woman," Marvin replied. "We didn't."

"Up yours, Marvin," said Cobb.

"Okay, what happened?" Marvin asked.

"I heard the Reilly boy was shot," Cobb said.

"Who the hell is the Reilly boy?"

Ben kept quiet and let the two old men go back and forth.

"Donny Reilly … his father owns the feed store out on Route 4."

"The boy that used to work at the drugstore?" Marvin asked.

"Yeah, that's him," Cobb said. "Agnes, over at the White Rose Diner, said that Marcia told her that it was a drug deal gone bad. Evidently the kid was a part of the robbery at the pharmacy."

"Ya don't say," Marvin replied. "I wonder if John Morgan was in on this? Ya know, I heard he was working undercover with the police department when he busted up that robbery."

Ben rolled his eyes and shook his head. "John wasn't working with the police department. He just happened to be walking by at the right time."

Cobb's smirked and nodded his head in Ben's direction. "Sounds like someone's a little jealous that John's getting all this attention."

"Yeah," Marvin added. "Claire said he was having a little trouble with it."

"When the hell did she tell you that?" Ben asked.

Cobb and Marvin both brayed like jackasses.

"Assholes," Ben said.

"Speaking of Claire," said Cobb, "who's her new friend in the fancy car?"

"What fancy car?" Ben asked.

"The Lincoln Town Car," Cobb responded. "It was here the other day, and then today she and Mica left in it."

Ben sat forward. "Left in it? What do you mean, left in it?"

"This morning I seen the car pull up, the guy went inside, and a little while later, Claire and Mica come out with him and got in the car and drove away."

Ben got up from his seat. "I have to go."

"Is everything okay?" Marvin asked.

"Yeah," Ben said. "Everything is fine. I just forgot something Claire wanted me to do." He walked down Marvin's steps and headed for the B&B. He could hear the phone ringing before he got to the door and picked up his pace.

"Hello?" Ben said.

"Max," Flannigan said, "I've been calling you all day."

"Where are they, Flannigan?" Ben demanded.

"They're here with me, Max … or Ben. Which would you prefer I call you?"

"If you hurt either one of them, I swear, I'll kill you and everyone you've ever cared about."

Flannigan let out a low, evil laugh. "Max, you're not in any position to make threats. You work for me now."

"I don't work for anyone," Ben argued.

"Listen, Max, I've already explained it. You bring me the man who killed my stepson, and you can have your new family back completely unharmed."

Ben cursed silently to himself. "It could take days to find this man."

"That's okay, Max, I have comfortable beds here for Claire and Mica. But don't take too long, because I can also dig a couple of comfortable holes in the ground."

"Where do I bring him when I find him?" Ben asked defeatedly.

"You can bring him to my home. Call when you have him and I'll give you the address. The clock is ticking, Max." Flannigan hung up.

There was a knock at the door and Ben spun around. John Morgan stood at the screen.

"Well, if it isn't the town hero, and just in time," Ben said.

"What do you mean?" John asked.

"Remember last night when we robbed that pharmacy?"

"Um, yeah, it was just last night."

"Well, tonight we have to break into the funeral home and steal a body."

"I don't want to be the town hero anymore," said John.

Chapter Eighteen

The Butler and Collins Funeral Home, the only funeral home in Dunquin Cove, sat at the corner of Shore Drive and Denton Street. Co-founders Alexander Collins and Alton Butler had died ages ago; Butler's grandson, Al, was now owner-operator. Al was in his late forties and had never married. The mortician was tall and gaunt, with a ghostly complexion and the creepily solicitous manner associated with persons of his vocation. He lived upstairs from the funeral home in a third floor, two-bedroom/one bath attic apartment.

"The door is locked," said John Morgan, gently wiggling the knob. The two men stood at the rear entrance of the old brick building, under a canvas canopy that read BUTLER AND COLLINS.

"Well, yeah," Ben replied. "Probably because it's one in the morning."

"We gotta make this quick. I told Jenny I would be home by two."

"Where did you tell her you were going?"

"The funeral home to steal a corpse."

"What! You told her that?"

"Yeah, we don't keep secrets from each other."

"So she knows it was really me that took down Snake and his crony at the pharmacy Monday night?"

"Well, I mean, we don't keep a lot of secrets from each other."

"That's what I thought." Ben stepped back away from the door and looked from window to window. He pointed at a window over a side entrance that Al used for flower deliveries. "Boost me up to that porch roof."

The two men walked around to the side of the building. John bent over and interlocked his fingers. Ben put his hand on John's shoulder and stepped into John's hands. John tossed him up to the roof with little effort.

Ben grabbed the edge, swung his leg up onto the roof, and pulled himself up. He went to the window; placing his fingertips against the glass he slid the sash upwards. He returned to the edge of the roof. He whispered down to John: "Go back to the door, I'll let you in."

John trotted back to the rear entrance. A few minutes later, Ben opened the door and let him inside. The duo went down a carpeted ramp into the basement where Al performed embalming and viewing prep; the space also served as storage for bodies during the winter months.

John pushed open the door to the embalming room. It let out an eerie creak, sending a chill up John's spine.

"Jesus," he whispered. "I don't know how anyone could do this for a living."

"Scared?" Ben asked.

"Scared of dead bodies in the basement of an old funeral home?" John asked. "Nah."

Ben raised his arms and made a woo-woo sound like a cartoon ghost.

"That's actually kinda scary when you do it down here."

Two bodies lay on separate stainless steel tables. Each body was covered from head to toe with a white cotton sheet.

"Which one we taking?" John asked.

"We'll take Elliott," Ben replied. He pulled back the corner of one of the sheets. It was the body of Donny Reilly. "Son of a bitch."

"Poor kid," John commented.

They both stood there for a minute staring at the young guy. Things for Donny didn't turn out the way Ben had wanted when he let him go at the drugstore. Ben slowly shook his head and tossed the sheet back over Donny's face.

John pointed at the other body. "Maybe that's Elliott."

Ben took hold of the corner of the sheet and lifted it a few inches. "Bingo," he said.

"Now what?" John asked.

"I was kinda hoping he would be in a body bag," Ben replied.

"Or at least be dressed," John added.

Ben looked around the room. "I wonder where they put his clothes."

John started opening drawers and doors looking for Elliott's personal belongings. "Here's a wallet, ring, and wristwatch." He held up a clear plastic bag.

"Let's have a look inside," said Ben.

John unzipped the bag and dumped the contents out on Elliott's chest. Ben reached for the wallet and opened it. "Douglas Elliott," he read aloud. "Five Linden Street, Boston, Massachusetts."

John found Elliott's clothing hung up in an oak wardrobe, removed them from their hangers, and the two men dressed Elliott.

"Should we roll him out of here on this table?" John asked. "It has wheels."

"Might as well," Ben replied. Together they wheeled him out of the embalming room and back up the ramp to the backdoor. They pushed the steel table across the parking lot and down a side driveway entrance to Denton Street where Ben's truck was parked. John waited in the driveway while Ben dropped the tailgate.

A spotlight lit up Ben's back and the bed of the truck.

Crap, John thought. He pulled the table back into the darkness against a house that sat to the right of the driveway. He pushed his back up against the side of the house, behind a bush, and held his breath.

"What's going on?" Chet Rose called out from his police cruiser. "Ben … is that you?"

Ben turned and shaded his eyes from the bright spotlight. "Hey, Chet, what's up?"

"Just making my rounds, Ben. Everything okay?" Chet left the car running and climbed out of his seat. "Truck break down?"

"Uh … just a flat tire," Ben said.

Chet looked at the tires he could see from where he stood. "Which one is it?"

"It was the back one there," he replied, pointing at the right rear passenger side tire. "I got it changed already. Just heading home."

"What brings you out this late?"

"We were playing cards down at The Cove. The game just let out a little while ago." Ben glanced to his right at John who stood motionless in the shadows.

"It looked like you were just opening your tailgate when I pulled up."

"Nope, just putting it up."

John moved his foot to the left and a twig cracked beneath his foot.

Chet's head snapped around; he pulled his flashlight from his utility belt. "Who's over there?" he called out.

John did his best to step in front of the table. "It's just me, Chet."

"What are you doing over there?"

"Taking a leak," John said. "You mind pointing that light in the other direction?"

"Oh sorry," said Chet.

John pretended to shake and zip his fly. He walked out onto the sidewalk. "How are you this evening, Chet?" he asked pleasantly.

"Good John, but I would appreciate it if you didn't pee on other people's houses."

"I had to go bad, and then the flat tire, and all."

Chet put the flashlight back in his utility belt. "I'm going to finish my rounds. You two have a nice evening."

"You too, Chet," said Ben. Both men gave Chet a half-wave. They stood their ground until Chet pulled away and turned down Lake Street.

"That was close," John said. He jogged back up the driveway and pulled the table to the truck. "You know, when Butler reports this body missing tomorrow, Chet will know why we were here, and he'll be asking a lot of questions."

"I was just changing a tire and you were just taking a leak," said Ben. "Stick to the story and everything will be fine."

"You always say everything will be fine, but then it never is."

Ben held up his finger. "One time," he said. "One little shootout."

John helped Ben lift Elliott into the back of the truck. "Can you really categorize any shootout as little?"

"Yes," Ben responded. "Anything less than eight bodies is considered little."

"Good to know," said John. "I learn so much from you."

Chapter Nineteen

"Are you sure you don't want me to go with you?" John asked.

Ben sat in his pickup truck in front of the Colsome House Bed and Breakfast. John stood outside the driver's side window. The sun hadn't come up yet, but the sky was turning a dark shade of orange and red in the east.

Ben stuck his hand out the truck window. "Thanks, pal, but I better do this one on my own."

John shook his hand and then slapped the roof of the old Ford pick-up. "All right, then."

Ben started the truck, put it in drive, and headed down Shore Drive. John watched until Ben's tail lights were out of sight. He glanced over at Alan Cobb's house. Cobb's porch light was on and he was standing on the front steps. He waved and then bent down to pick up the Sunday morning edition of the *Dunquin Crier*.

"Morning, Cobb," John said.

"Morning, John," Cobb replied. "What brings you out this early?"

"Just seeing Ben off this morning. He's driving down to Boston for the day."

"What's he got going on in Boston?"

"He's just delivering a package for a guy."

"Ah." Cobb nodded his head. "Cup of coffee?"

John looked up Shore Drive one way and down the other. "You know, I think I will have a cup. Thanks, Cobb."

"It's the least I can do for Dunquin Cove's newest hero."

"Yeah, hero," John mumbled.

*****

Ben got off I-95 at exit 46 and pulled into a Dunkin Donuts. He shut off the truck and went inside.

"Can I help you?" asked the young pimply faced kid behind the counter.

"Medium coffee with cream and sugar," Ben replied.

The kid poked at buttons on the register with his index finger. "Medium?" he asked.

"Yes."

"Is that an iced coffee?"

"No."

"Hot coffee," the kid said to himself. "You want sugar in that?"

"Yes. Sugar and cream."

The kid jabbed at a few more buttons. "And you said, cream?"

"Yes."

"Two forty-nine, please."

Ben placed a five-dollar bill on the counter. "Keep the change," he said.

"Thanks, mister."

"Is there a pay phone around here?" Ben asked.

"A pay phone?"

"Yeah. It's a phone and you pay to use it."

"I know what it is, but I don't know if there is one around here."

"You got a cell phone I can use?"

"Yes."

"Can I use it for a second?"

The kid cocked his head. "I don't know," he said slowly. "I don't like other people using my phone."

"I just gave you a two dollar tip."

"That was for coffee, not for my phone."

"Here ya go, sir," said a young girl at the pick-up station. She set Ben's coffee on the counter.

Ben turned back to Pimples. "How much would it cost me to use your phone?" he asked.

Pimples didn't hesitate. "Ten bucks."

Ben pulled a ten out of his money clip and tossed it on the counter. The kid handed him the cell. Ben pulled a folded yellow Post-it note out of his pocket and dialed the number that was written on it.

After the third ring, Flannigan said, "Hello?"

"Flannigan, it's Ben Dunning."

"Good morning, Ben. You're calling early. How can I help you?"

"I found the guy who killed your stepson."

There was a few seconds of silence and then Flannigan said, "Very efficient. Where is he now?"

"He's with me."

"What's his name?"

"I'll tell you that when I bring him to you. Where am I bringing him?"

"My home, 41 Chestnut Street. My wife is out of town."

"Are Claire and Mica with you?"

"Yes, they are, and quite anxious for you to arrive."

"I'll be there in twenty minutes." Ben hung up the cell and tossed it on the counter in front of the kid. "I would delete that number if I were you, kid."

Ben picked up his coffee and went out the door. When he got outside, he saw an elderly man and woman looking into the bed of his truck.

"Can I help you?" Ben called out.

"Is this guy okay?" the old man asked, as he stared at Elliott's dead body.

"He'll be fine," Ben replied.

"What's a matter with him?"

"Lead poisoning," Ben said.

Chapter Twenty

Ben pulled to the curb on Chestnut Street and shut off his engine. The sidewalk and street, the tops of vehicles, and leaves of the crab apple trees that lined the street were wet with morning dew. Ben rolled down his window and filled his lungs with the crisp morning air. He could see Flannigan's front door from where he sat, two doors down.

Flannigan lived in a brick town house in the affluent neighborhood of Beacon Hill, a couple of blocks from Boston Common. A man in a dark suit stood on Flannigan's stoop. A cigarette hung from the corner of his mouth. He had his hands in his pockets to keep them warm. The man probably hadn't planned on this cold of a morning this early in the year.

Ben leaned over, popped open the glove box, and grabbed hold of his 9mm. He climbed out of the truck—keeping his eye on Flannigan's door thug the entire time—and stuffed the gun between his waistband and the small of his back. He walked to the rear of the truck and opened the tailgate.

Ben grabbed Elliott's body by the ankles and slid him out of the truck bed. He turned him onto his back and lifted the dead man onto his left shoulder. He walked down the sidewalk as if he was taking his dog for a morning stroll.

"Good morning," Ben said to the door thug.

"What the hell?" asked the man.

"I'm here to see Flannigan."

"Is that man dead?"

"Open the door," Ben grunted. "He's getting heavy."

The man started to turn. "I'll let him know you're here."

Ben yanked the gun from his waistband and trained it on the man. "Just open the friggin' door."

"Not gonna happen." The goon pulled a small walkie-talkie from his inside jacket pocket.

Ben pointed the gun at the man's leg. "You can open it healthy, or you can open it with a limp. Your choice."

"What?"

Ben shot the door thug in the thigh. He fell backwards with a sharp cry and caught himself on the wrought iron railing.

"That's bleeding pretty badly already," Ben said. "You're going to want to get inside and call for an ambulance." Ben knew he only had minutes now that he had fired his weapon. He walked up the steps, his gun still on the man. "You going to unlock that door, or should I get the other leg?"

The guy put up his hand. "Wait," he said. "I'll unlock it."

When the door was unlocked, Ben stepped into the foyer, his gun still in his hand, hanging at his side. The wounded man limped in past him and into the living room. He had his hand on his thigh, applying pressure. Flannigan was standing at the top of the stairs.

"His name is Douglas Elliott," said Ben. He dumped the body unceremoniously on the marble tile floor.

"You killed him?" Flannigan asked. "I wanted him alive."

Ben rubbed his aching shoulder. "He was a small-time drug dealer from Dorchester. I don't know what business your stepson had with him. That's something you can look into on your own."

"Mr. Flannigan," said the door thug, "I need to see a doctor."

Flannigan glowered at him unsympathetically. "Shut up, Vince." His eyes went back to Ben. "I wanted to kill him."

"Sorry. Where's Claire and Mica?"

"Mr. Flannigan," said Vince. The color was leaving his face. "Mr. Flannigan." He tumbled forward and landed unconscious on an Oriental rug in the center of the room. Blood continued to spill out of his leg.

Flannigan shook his head in disgust. "I'll never get that stain out," he said.

"Where are they?" Ben asked.

"Claire!" Flannigan shouted. "Grab that boy and get out here."

Ben heard a door open. Claire walked to the top of the stairs near Flannigan; she was holding Mica's hand.

"Come on, Claire," Ben said, "we have to go … now."

Claire walked past Flannigan and down the stairs. When she got to the bottom she stepped over Elliott's body. She tried to put her arms around Ben.

Ben heard sirens off in the distance. "Later," he said. He grabbed Claire by the hand and pulled her through the house and out the back door. He led his family down the steps, through the neighbor's backyard, and out onto Willow Street. They rounded the corner onto Chestnut, where Ben's truck was parked.

Ben opened the door for Claire. She helped Mica into the truck and climbed in behind him. No one spoke as Ben got into the driver's seat, started the engine, and drove away. When they were almost to Cedar Street, Ben glanced in the rearview mirror to see two Boston patrol cars rounding the corner, lights flashing and sirens blaring.

Ben took a left onto Charles Street and headed for home.

Chapter Twenty-One

The ride back to Dunquin Cove was mostly quiet. Claire assured Ben they hadn't been harmed physically. Psychological damage, now that was another beast entirely. And not all of it came from the abduction. His family knew he had killed a man and critically injured another. Trauma would rear its ugly head in both subtle and overt ways. His jaw clenched in expectation of the worst.

Ben pulled into the driveway of the B&B at few minutes after nine on Sunday morning. He pulled around and parked in front of the garage. Mica was asleep, so Ben gently slid him out of the seat and carried him up to his room. He put Mica in bed and tucked the blankets around the young boy's shoulders. The activity had awaken him.

"Thanks for coming and getting us," Mica whispered. "Mom was scared, but I told her there was nothing to worry about. I told her you would come for us."

Ben leaned over, pushed Mica's bangs to the side, and kissed him on the forehead. "Get some sleep, little buddy."

When Ben got to the bottom of the stairs he could hear water running in the kitchen. When he walked in, Claire was standing with her back to him, filling the sink with water. "I have to get these dishes done," she said. She shut off the faucet and turned around. Her hands were trembling and tears filled her eyes. Ben moved closer and put his arms around her. "You're okay," he said. "Everything is going to be okay."

Claire began sobbing. Her shoulders shook. "Did you kill that man?" she asked.

"Yes."

"You killed him to get us back?"

"No. I killed him yesterday morning … before you were taken."

Claire stepped back and looked up into Ben's eyes. "Then why—"

 "He was a drug dealer."

"And the man you shot in the leg at Flannigan's?"

"He probably died as well."

"How many men have you killed?" Claire asked

"You mean, *this* week?" Ben asked.

The End

Coming Soon:

High Maintenance

From Fernandina Beach Mysteries

Excited About Nothing

Jake Stellar Series

ALSO BY RODNEY RIESEL

From the Tales of Dan Coast Series

Sleeping Dogs Lie
Ocean Floors
The Coast of Christmas Past
Ship of Fools
Double Trouble
Most Likely to Die
Deadly Moves
On the Wagon
No Enemies Here

Jake Stellar Series

North Murder Beach
Beach Shoot
When Death Returns
The Obedience of Fools
Dead in the Water

The Dunquin Cove Series

The Man in Room Number Four
Return to Dunquin Cove

Sunrise City Series
Sunrise City
Sunrise City 2: From Bad to Worse
Never Strikes Twice

Fernandina Beach Mysteries

Maintenance Required

From Here to There: A Collection of Short Stories